The Secret of
the Lion's Head

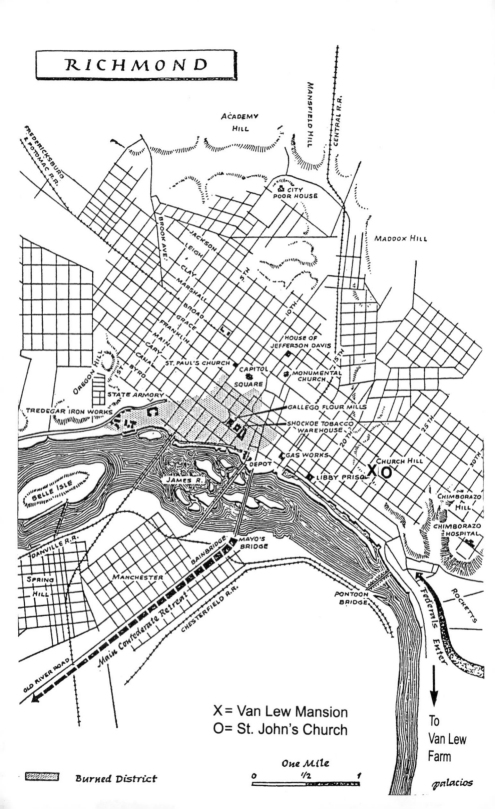

RICHMOND

ACADEMY HILL

MANSFIELD HILL

CENTRAL R.R.

FREDERICKSBURG & POTOMAC R.R.

CITY POOR HOUSE

MADDOX HILL

BROOK AVE.

JACKSON
LEIGH
CLAY
MARSHALL
BROAD
GRACE
FRANKLIN
MAIN
CARY
CANAL

5TH
5TH
10TH

HOUSE OF JEFFERSON DAVIS

15TH

ST. PAUL'S CHURCH

CAPITOL SQUARE

MONUMENTAL CHURCH

OREGON HILL

ST. BYRD

STATE ARMORY

GALLEGO FLOUR MILLS

SHOCKOE TOBACCO WAREHOUSE

TREDEGAR IRON WORKS

GAS WORKS

20TH

25TH

30TH

CHURCH HILL

X O

DEPOT

LIBBY PRISON

JAMES R.

BELLE ISLE

CHIMBORAZO HILL

CHIMBORAZO HOSPITAL

DANVILLE R.R.

BAINBRIDGE

MAYO'S BRIDGE

SPRING HILL

MANCHESTER

PONTOON BRIDGE

ROCKETTS

CHESTERFIELD R.R.

Main Confederate Retreat

OLD RIVER ROAD

Federals Enter

To Van Lew Farm

X = Van Lew Mansion
O = St. John's Church

Burned District

One Mile
0   1/2   1

palacios

The Secret of the Lion's Head

Beverly B. Hall

White Mane Publishing Company, Inc.
Shippensburg, Pennsylvania

This White Mane Publishing Company, Inc. publication was printed by
Beidel Printing House, Inc.
63 West Burd Street
Shippensburg, PA 17257 USA

In respect for the scholarship contained herein, the acid-free paper used in this book meets the guidelines for permanence and durability of the Committee on Production Guidelines for Book Longevity of the Council on Library Resources.

For a complete list of available publications please write
White Mane Publishing Company, Inc.
P.O. Box 152
Shippensburg, PA 17257 USA

Library of Congress Cataloging-in-Publication Data

Hall, Beverly B., 1918-
    The secret of the lion's head / Beverly B. Hall.
        p.   cm.
    Summary: Living with her aunt in Richmond during the Civil War, Annie notices mysterious goings on and suspects that Auntie Elizabeth is a Union spy.
    ISBN 0-942597-92-3 (alk. paper)
    1. Van Lew, Elizabeth L., 1818-1900--Juvenile fiction. 2. United States--History--Civil War, 1861-1865--Juvenile fiction. [1. Van Lew, Elizabeth L., 1818-1900--Fiction. 2. United States--History--Civil War, 1861-1865--Fiction. 3. Spies--Fiction. 4. Aunts--Fiction.] I. Title.
PZ7.H14112Se   1995
[Fic]--dc20   95-30202
                                                              CIP
                                                              AC

PRINTED IN THE UNITED STATES OF AMERICA

Dedicated to my husband, Randolph
Van Lew Hall, Annie's grandson, and
to the memory of our granddaughter,
Elizabeth Van Lew Kern

Table of Contents

Chapter 1

"Crazy Bett! Crazy Bett!
Bet the Yankees get you yet!"

Annie Van Lew could hear the chanting of the boys as they pranced along Grace Street, splattering mud in all directions. They were following a small woman who was dressed in a shabby black cape, muddy boots, and an enormous brown bonnet that almost completely hid her face. The day was a bright one in February 1865, but she clutched her cloak tightly about her in the cold wind. She carried an empty basket on one arm. Her head was tipped to one side and she muttered and sang to herself as she scurried along the brick sidewalk.

When the strange figure neared the house, Annie bounced down the curving steps that led from the first floor porch. She hurried to open the gate with a happy smile of greeting. The small woman ducked under the porch and disappeared through a door that led into the basement.

The boys were still milling around in the street, undecided as to what to do now that the object of their teasing was no longer in sight. Annie leaned on the gate, watching. One of the boys made a face at her, and the others began chanting again. Annie's face flushed with anger as she listened.

"Crazy Bett! Crazy Bett! Crazy, crazy, crazy!"

"She is not crazy! She's my aunt!" Annie shouted in helpless rage.

Someone threw a mudball at her, and she ducked, but it fell short. The boys whooped and laughed, then started running down the street. One of them dragged a stick along the fence, adding to the racket. Annie stuck her tongue out at their backs. That made her feel better, even if they couldn't see it.

Inside the house, she climbed the stairs to her aunt's bedroom. She knocked softly on the half-opened door.

"Auntie ..."

"Come in, Annie dear." Elizabeth Van Lew was seated at her dressing table, brushing her blonde hair with a monogrammed silver brush. She wore a blue silk dressing gown, and tiny brocaded slippers. There was no sign of the cloak and boots and bonnet that she had worn just a few minutes earlier.

Annie plopped down in a big wing chair with embroidered upholstery and returned her aunt's loving glance with a smile.

Then she scowled. "I wish those boys didn't yell at you like that."

"Nonsense. It doesn't bother me a bit," Aunt Elizabeth said.

"It's not fair! You're not crazy!"

"I know that, and you know that. What a gang of street boys thinks about me doesn't matter."

Annie stared out of one of the large windows that overlooked the garden and walkways that sloped down to the James River, sparkling in the late afternoon sun. "But you do dress funny when you go out," she said hesitantly.

"Perhaps. I think it's sensible. You wouldn't expect me to walk around muddy streets in these slippers, would you?"

"Of course not!" Annie giggled. "I remember when my shoe came untied once and came off in the mud. I took my sock off too! It felt so good squishing between my toes! But it wasn't cold out like today."

Aunt Elizabeth put down her hairbrush and walked over to the wardrobe in one corner of the room. "I'm going to dress now, Annie. You run along and send Dorcas to help me, please. And see if you can find Eliza. It's almost time to clean up for supper."

Annie delivered the message to Dorcas, the black maid, then went looking for her little sister. She found Eliza in a corner of the carriage house, playing with a box of kittens.

"Oh Annie, look! This one has four white paws and a white tip to her tail!" Eliza said. "Isn't she pretty!"

Annie dropped down beside her and reached into the box. "I like this big tiger one," she said. She lifted the kitten into her lap and he began to bat at the end of one of her long brown ringlets. "Auntie says it's time to wash for supper. You'll have to come in now."

Eliza pouted. "I want to play with the kittens some more. Auntie is always telling me what to do! I wish we didn't have to live here anymore. Annie, when are Mama and Papa coming back?"

Annie dropped the kitten back into the box and gave her little sister a quick hug. "You know Mama's never coming back, Eliza," she said. "She died and went to heaven three years ago when I was seven, just like you. I guess you were too young to remember. I was scared and sad and I cried." Annie seldom admitted being scared, even to herself, but she still remembered her panic. She had wondered what would happen to her without Mama.

"Did Papa go to heaven too?"

"No, silly! Papa went to war. He's a soldier in the Union army, and he can't come home till the war is over, 'cause we live in Richmond and it's Confederate."

"What's Confederate?"

"I don't know, exactly. Except that the Confederates keep slaves and want to be a separate country and not part of the United States anymore. Papa and Auntie set their slaves free, and want Virginia to stay in the Union. Anyway, Auntie is taking care of us until Papa comes home, so we have to do as she says, just as if she were our mama." Annie scrambled to her feet and reached out her hand to her little sister. "Come on, let's get ready to eat. I'm hungry!"

As they ran across the yard, Annie saw a figure dart from the basement door. To her surprise she saw that it was Dorcas, Aunt Elizabeth's maid. Inside the house, Annie glanced quickly at the row of hooks by the door. She was right! Auntie's cloak and bonnet were gone. And Dorcas had been wearing them.

──Chapter 2

The next morning Annie sat alone at the big mahogany table in the dining room, hungrily eating her breakfast of corn meal mush. Eliza had already finished and run off to see her beloved kittens. Aunt Elizabeth was nowhere in sight. Annie took a drink of hot chocolate from her own special blue cup and wondered again about Dorcas.

The maid had a thick brown coat of her own, so she didn't need Auntie's cloak to keep warm when she went out. Try as she might, Annie couldn't think of any reason why Dorcas would have borrowed the shabby black cloak and big ugly bonnet. They certainly weren't pretty! And where had she been going alone at dusk? The streets weren't safe for anyone at night in Richmond in this fourth year of war. Aunt Elizabeth had told her that soldiers or thieves would kill for a pair of boots or a warm coat.

Deep inside, Annie had a feeling she should tell Auntie what she'd seen, but she liked Dorcas, and she didn't want her to get in trouble. She remembered several times when Dorcas had kept quiet

6

about some of Annie's escapades and saved her from scoldings and punishment.

Annie stirred her chocolate with a heavy silver spoon and frowned at the gilt-framed oil painting on the wall. It was a hunting scene, and she hated it because it showed men killing a beautiful deer.

"If you aren't careful your face will freeze like that, Miss Annie. You want to grow up looking like a bad dream?"

"Dorcas! I didn't hear you come in!" Annie stared at the stains on the tablecloth where her chocolate had spattered. "Look at the mess I made when I jumped!"

"I didn't mean to startle you," Dorcas said. "And don't worry about the tablecloth. I came in to see if you were finished with your breakfast so I could take the linens to Bessie for laundering."

Annie tipped her head back to drain the last of her drink from the cup, then wiped the chocolate mustache from her lips. "All done! But now my napkin looks as bad as the cloth!" She giggled. "And how could my face freeze when I'm inside and warm?"

"Never you mind how! What's bothering you that you need to scowl like that anyway?"

"Where's Aunt Elizabeth?"

"Out." Dorcas finished moving the empty dishes to a tray on the sideboard and rolled up the dirty linen.

"Out where?"

"That's not my business, or yours, Miss Annie."

Annie slid down from her chair and started to follow the black woman toward the door.

"Then I guess it isn't her business where you were last night," she said slowly.

She stopped as Dorcas whirled around in the doorway, her dark eyes narrow, her face empty-looking.

"What do you mean, Miss Annie? Where was I last night? What are you talking about?"

"Well, I don't know exactly where you went ... but I saw you going out when Eliza and I were coming in for supper." She hesitated for a moment, then decided to go ahead and ask the question that had been bothering her. "Why were you wearing Aunt Elizabeth's cloak and bonnet?"

Dorcas laughed, but it was a strange sort of cackle, nothing at all like her usual musical laughter.

"Oh, that! Nothing strange about that! Miss Lizzie sent me on an errand and told me to wear her things. Said I'd be safer than in my own good coat. Now you go get Miss 'Liza and get upstairs for schooling. Miss Lizzie left your lessons all ready for you."

Annie stared after Dorcas who hurried toward the back stairs leading to the basement. She was certainly acting peculiar. Almost as if she didn't want to stay around a minute longer than she had to.

Upstairs in the library, Annie leaned her elbows on the big table and rested her chin in her hands. Eliza sat opposite her, her blonde curls bobbing up and down as she practiced forming her letters, the tip of her pink tongue sticking out of the corner of her mouth as she concentrated. Annie sighed. She couldn't keep her mind on her arithmetic problems.

Why did Dorcas act so strange, she wondered. Everything seemed as usual between us until I asked her about her actions last night. Dorcas has always been friendly and seemed to like having me follow her around and talk to her. I hope she doesn't stay angry. It's lonely enough already in this big house with no friends to play with.

Annie jumped to her feet and walked over to one of the library's tall windows. The Van Lew mansion and grounds took up a whole block on Grace Street, between 23rd and 24th streets, and went down almost to the river in back. Kitty-corner across the street was St. John's Episcopal Church. Patrick Henry was supposed to have delivered his famous speech about "Give me liberty or give me death!" there, back before the Revolution. The Van Lews still went to that church, but people seldom spoke to them anymore.

Annie craned her neck and looked out over the area known as Church Hill. There were lots of children in the neighborhood, but they weren't allowed to play with her and Eliza. Auntie had explained that it was because the Van Lews were for the Union and against slavery. Papa was fighting on the wrong side in this war between the states. But understanding didn't help when Annie was so lonely. If only she had a friend her own age to talk to! She'd seen Confederate President Jefferson Davis' daughter Margaret once when she was walking with her mother and little brothers near the Executive Mansion. She was about Annie's age, and they called her Maggie. Maybe she'd have made a good friend.

"Annie, PLEASE!"

"Sorry, Eliza. What did you say?" She jerked her attention back to the library.

"I asked you twice! Please listen to my spelling."

"Not now. If you've finished, go play with the stupid kittens. I have to do my own work!" She stood there and watched Eliza's blue eyes fill with tears. Her little sister snuffled loudly as she ran from the room.

"Eliza!" Annie called. Then she sighed. She knew she'd been mean, but she didn't care. In a fit of temper she picked up her arithmetic book and threw it across the room at the fireplace. It hit with a good hard thud, right on the head of one of the lions that topped the columns on either side.

She heard Aunt Elizabeth's voice in the hallway below, and dashed to get her book before she was caught neglecting her studies. She didn't want the extra lessons that would surely follow daydreaming during school hours. Then she stopped and stared at the lion's head in surprise. Now it was turned sideways. It hadn't broken, just twisted when her book hit it. Behind the lion's head was a small space that seemed to have something in it.

——Chapter 3

As Annie peered into the space behind the lion's head, she heard Aunt Elizabeth's light footsteps tripping up the stairs. She grabbed her book and hurried back to the big library table. When Auntie came into the room, Annie was sitting with her back to the fireplace, arithmetic book open in front of her and pencil in hand. She hoped Auntie wouldn't ask to see what she'd done so far this morning.

"Good morning, Annie. Almost finished with your arithmetic?"

"Not quite. I was late getting started today." She wasn't exactly lying, even if she really hadn't started at all yet. "I'll be done before very long." She was glad arithmetic was easy for her and she could hurry through it if she had to.

"Good. I have a treat for you later." Aunt Elizabeth walked across the room and placed one of the lamps she was carrying on the mantle. Annie held her breath, waiting for her to say something about the lion, but her aunt turned and placed the other lamp on the table between the rear windows. Annie was careful not to look toward the fireplace.

"What kind of treat, Auntie?" She bounced a little in her chair with excitement. "Something to eat or something to do?"

Auntie smiled at her. "Both. When your school-work is done, go change into some old, warm clothes. It's a beautiful day, and I thought we'd hitch up Chieftain to the wagon and take a trip out to the farm. Cook is packing us some food to eat on the way. We'll leave as soon as you're ready."

"I'll hurry! I'll hurry!" Annie exclaimed. The farm was one of her favorite places. "Don't go without me!"

Aunt Elizabeth laughed. "No danger of that!" She left the room and Annie heard her go into her bed-room and close the door.

For a minute she sat quietly, in case Auntie came back, then she turned around to face the fireplace. To her surprise it looked just as it always did, with the lion facing straight ahead. The lamp with its newly-cleaned chimney sat in its usual spot, and the brass clock in the middle ticked away between the china figurines. There was no sign that anything had moved.

"I know I didn't imagine it," Annie said to her-self. "I know the lion moved!" She hopped out of her chair and walked over to the fireplace. She exam-ined both lions very carefully. The one on the left was solid and sturdy and looked as if it were all in one piece with the column beneath it. But the one on the right showed a tiny hairline crack in the paint, so small it couldn't be seen unless one looked for it.

She glanced anxiously at the library door, then reached out and gave the lion's head a push. Nothing happened. She tried again, a little harder. Still nothing. She stood on one foot, rubbing her other shoe on the back of her leg, and bit her lower lip, thinking hard. The book had hit the lion's head at an angle, down near where it joined the column. If she pushed in the same place...She gave the head a slight twist and it moved easily, revealing the space behind it. But this time the hole was empty. There was no trace of whatever it was that she'd seen in it before. It had looked like a piece of white paper, but now there was nothing. She squeezed her hand into the hole and felt around with her fingers. Empty.

Carefully she turned the lion's head back so it looked untouched and went back to her chair, back to those arithmetic problems. Auntie must have closed the hole when she put the lamp on the mantle, but why hadn't she said anything about it? Did Aunt Elizabeth know what had happened to the paper?

"I can't think about that now," Annie said to herself. "If I don't get these problems done I may not get to go to the farm! And it's been a long time since I was there last — way last October, at harvest time. Sometimes I wish we could live there instead of the city. It's always so noisy and crowded here!"

Bending her head over her paper she put her mind to her arithmetic and rushed to solve the problems as fast as she could.

I won't bother to check my answers today, she decided. I don't make many mistakes, and checking will take too long.

She closed the book with a snap and ran from the library to her bedroom across the hall. Rapidly she changed into a red plaid flannel dress and her sturdy outdoor boots, then clattered down the stairs to the basement entrance to get her wool cloak and bonnet. If she hurried she might get to the stables in time to help harness Chieftain.

──Chapter 4

At the stable Annie found Chieftain already hitched to the wagon. A happier-looking Eliza was perched on the seat, and Aunt Elizabeth was putting her basket in the back. "Hop in, Annie," she said gaily. She climbed up next to Eliza and picked up the reins. "We're off for an outing in the country, tra-la," she sang in a pleasant low voice. "And we won't be home until dark, tra-la! What fun! What fun! What fun!"

Annie and Eliza looked at each other and grinned. Auntie hadn't been in a mood to laugh and play with them for a long time, and they were going to enjoy every minute of it. As the wagon went down the 24th Street hill toward the river and turned left onto Main Street, they joined her in making up silly songs and singing old favorites. Annie started to sing Yankee Doodle, but Auntie stopped her quickly. "Not here and now, Annie! That's a Yankee song, and the Confederates don't like to hear it!"

The road followed the river toward the southeast. They were traveling through the district known as Rocketts, the dock area of Richmond. Confederate soldiers had a large camp near there, and there were several old tobacco warehouses, the Confederate Navy Yard, and an army supply warehouse. It was a noisy, busy, dirty place that smelled awful, and was filled with soldiers, sailors, workingmen, cannons, and army wagons.

Annie didn't like that part of town, and she wished they could travel faster and get through the area more quickly. She knew it wasn't safe for a little girl to go there alone, but she wasn't afraid driving through with Aunt Elizabeth.

The wagon rattled and bumped along. How well Auntie manages the driving, Annie thought. Her hands were strong and firm on the reins, and Chieftain was well-behaved, even though Annie knew he'd love to run and run after being shut up in the stable for several days. Something puzzled her though.

"Auntie, you drive so well, but you don't do it much. Why didn't Ben come along to do the driving for us?"

"Ben had other work to do today. And where would we put him? There's only room for the three of us on the seat. You could ride in the back going out to the farm, but there won't be any space there when we come home."

"What are we going to put there?" asked Eliza.

"Food, silly," answered Annie. "If we couldn't get food from our farm we wouldn't have enough to eat. People are starving in Richmond 'cause things cost so much, Dorcas told me."

"She's right," Auntie said. "Prices are so high because there's a shortage. There are soldiers and sailors and prisoners to be fed, as well as all the freed slaves, and refugees from the battle areas. There just isn't enough food to go around, what with the Union blockade and the soldiers on both sides stealing from the farms. We're lucky our farm is still safe."

"I'm hungry," said Eliza. "I always get hungry when I think about food. When are we going to eat?"

"Soon, now. We're already out of the city, and I know a pleasant spot along the river where we can stop, about half a mile ahead." Aunt Elizabeth made little clucking noises and slapped the reins. Chieftain stepped out faster.

A few minutes later Auntie turned the wagon off onto a little rutted lane and pulled up near a small grove of trees. Right away Annie noticed a large grassy spot nearby where they could sit in the sun and watch all the boats moving up and down the river.

While Aunt Elizabeth tethered Chieftain to a tree, Annie lifted the basket from the back of the wagon and took out the checkered cloth that was folded over the top. She spread this out on the ground, weighting the corners down with some stones so it wouldn't blow away in the breeze from the river. She set out the plates and cups and eating utensils, then unpacked the food.

"Oh, goody! Fried chicken!" squealed Eliza as she watched Annie. "I _love_ chicken!"

"Me too," said Annie. "And look — there's cabbage slaw and cornbread. This is a real feast, Auntie!"

Aunt Elizabeth poured cold buttermilk from a covered jar into their cups. "I told you it would be a treat! I asked Cook to use these things since we'll be getting more from the farm today. And it's almost spring, so it won't be long before the fresh things are growing again."

When they had finished their meal, Annie reached into the basket and brought out yet another cloth-wrapped package. "And here's dessert!" she said as she opened it. To her delight it held small fried fruit pies, one for each, made from dried peaches.

She licked the crumbs from her fingers, and stared dreamily at the river. Where were all the boats and barges going? Someday, when the war was over, she'd get on a boat and go somewhere. Europe, or China, maybe. There was so much of the world out there she'd like to see.

Aunt Elizabeth began gathering up the dishes. "Come on, girls, we still have several miles to go, so we'd better get started. Annie, untie Chieftain and lead him around so we're headed back out to the road."

As Annie turned the wagon around, she gave Chieftain some gentle pats on the side of the neck. She felt sorry for the big brown horse. He was a Kentucky-bred saddle horse and had never had to pull things before. But the soldiers had come through and taken all the other horses, including the chestnuts that pulled the carriage. They had missed Chieftain because Aunt Elizabeth was out riding him when they came. Now he was the only one left to pull the heavy wagon.

This time Aunt Elizabeth put Annie in the middle of the wagon seat. When they turned onto the main road again, she handed the reins to her. "Here you go, Annie. You drive the rest of the way to the farm. It will be good practice for you, and quite safe now that we're out of the city crowds."

Annie beamed with pride. She loved to drive, and seldom had the chance. What a wonderful trip this was! And ahead of them, only about three miles more, was the farm, where there was always something interesting and exciting to do.

——Chapter 5

As Annie turned the wagon onto the side road leading to the farmhouse she noticed that most of the fields were already plowed and ready for seeding. She hoped it would be a good year, or they might all be hungry next winter.

They drove into the farmyard. "Look, Auntie! There's Matt by the barn," Annie said. "He looks as if he's waiting for us!"

"He is. I sent a message several days ago that we'd be here today if the weather was good. I want to go over plans for this year with him as well as get some food. You girls will have several hours to play, but don't stray too far. We want to get home by dark."

Annie liked Matt Bowser because he was big and jolly and he liked to have the children visit. Once he'd been a slave, but Auntie had given him his freedom. Now he was the farm manager.

"Miss Annie! Miss 'Liza!" Matt called. "You're both lookin' mighty fine! Guess all our farm food agrees with you. You ain't gettin' much taller, though, Miss Annie," he teased, "even if you do drive a wagon pretty good!"

"I know," she sighed. "When Auntie measured me against the wall last week I hadn't grown at all since last August. I suppose I'm always going to be short, like Auntie is. I wish I could be tall like Mary!"

"Oh! I almost forgot!" Matt grinned at her. "Mary's here today and she has ginger cookies and milk for you in the kitchen. Run along now, while I take care of Chieftain."

The farmhouse kitchen was warm and smelled of freshly baked bread, ginger cookies, and some kind of savory stew that was steaming on the back of the big wood-burning stove. Matt's daughter, Mary, was all smiles as she served the milk and cookies.

"My, it's nice to see you girls again! I was hoping you'd come on a day when I was here."

"Me too," said Annie. "I love coming to the farm, but I wish we could see you in Richmond too."

Mary laughed. "Not much chance of that! I'm kept too busy at the Presidential Mansion, and you know Miss Lizzie and Mrs. Davis don't have anything to do with each other!"

"Why not?" asked Eliza.

"Because they're on opposite sides in the war, silly," answered Annie. "Mr. Davis is the Confederate President, and you know Papa and Auntie are Union. Mr. Lincoln is <u>our</u> President!"

Eliza seemed bewildered. "Then why does Mary work for them instead of us?"

Annie looked at the black girl questioningly, but she had turned away. Why _did_ Mary work for the Confederate President? Now that Eliza had mentioned it, it did seem very strange.

"I don't know," she said slowly. "Maybe it's because we already have Dorcas. Is that why, Mary?"

"That's a pretty good reason," Mary answered. But it seemed to Annie that Mary was acting like Dorcas had this morning. Almost as if they didn't want to answer Annie's questions. Sometime she was going to have to try to figure it all out, but not right now.

"Come on, Eliza. Let's go outdoors and play while we can." She brushed cookie crumbs from her chin as she headed toward the door. "Thank you, Mary," she called as she went out. "We'll see you before we go."

Annie glanced over her shoulder as they ran across the barnyard, but Matt and Aunt Elizabeth were nowhere in sight. The girls headed toward the orchard for the swing that was there just for them.

They had a wonderful, long afternoon. They played in the hay, cuddled the baby chickens, and searched for eggs. They climbed the smallest apple tree, then chased the big dog and threw sticks for him to fetch. When he trotted down to the brook, they followed him and tried looking for frogs. They were tired and happy and dirty by the time they got back to the wagon. Matt had just finished loading it with food supplies.

"I don't know how we'd manage without you and the farm," Aunt Elizabeth was saying. "The prices in Richmond are outrageous! Twenty dollars for a pound of butter or bacon, and fifty dollars for a live hen! Of course, that's Confederate money," she added scornfully. "No one in the South has any real American money anymore."

Annie looked in the back of the wagon. She was glad to see the sacks of flour and tubs of lard, butter and cheese, cabbages, strings of dried beans, and bags of potatoes. There were jugs of cider, smoked hams, sausages, bacon, and a crate of live chickens. It looked like enough food for a long time, but she knew there were lots of mouths to feed. Not only would this be used by the Van Lew household, but every day or so Auntie took a basket of food to the Union army officers who were in Libby Prison down by the river, just a short walk from home.

She said goodbye to Mary and Matt and climbed up next to Aunt Elizabeth. Eliza sat on the other side with a big basket of eggs at her feet. There was a similar basket on Annie's side, and she reached down to steady it as the wagon lurched forward. One of the eggs started to roll off, and she grabbed it before it could fall. To her surprise it felt very light — not at all like a regular egg. She straightened up on the seat with the egg in her hand. While Auntie was busy guiding Chieftain out onto the farm road, Annie looked at the egg carefully. It had a small hole in one end, and all the insides were gone.

Why would Matt or Mary have put an empty eggshell in our basket, she wondered. I've never seen a shell that was empty but still in one piece. Usually they're broken in half, like I break my breakfast eggs. Why would anyone want to empty an eggshell so carefully that it didn't break?

──Chapter 6

Aunt Elizabeth turned the wagon onto the main road leading home. Eliza was chattering about the things they'd done and the fun they'd had.

"You're very quiet, Annie," Auntie said. "Not too tired from our outing, I hope?"

"No," Annie said slowly. "Not tired." She hesitated a moment, then decided to ask about the egg. "But I am curious." She held out the eggshell. "Did you ever see anything like this, Auntie?"

"Well of course! It's an egg. We have two baskets of them right here. You know what eggs are, Annie!"

"But this just looks like an egg." She turned it around to show the hole in the end. "The insides are all gone. How would that happen? And why would somebody do that and then give us the shell?"

"Maybe snakes did it," suggested Eliza. "I heard that snakes like to suck eggs."

"Snakes wouldn't put it in our basket, silly!" Annie said. "And if Matt or Mary put it there they'd know it was empty. I noticed right away that it was too light for an egg. That's probably why it started to roll off when we began to move. If I hadn't caught it, it would have smashed on the floor."

Aunt Elizabeth smiled. "Well if it had, at least we wouldn't have wasted a real egg. Let me take it, Annie, and we'll dispose of it when we get home. Broken shells are good to scatter in the pens for the chickens to scratch up. They don't have teeth, you know, so they need to eat sand and gravel and such things to grind up the food in their gizzards." She put the shell in her reticule.

"Ugh!" said Eliza. "I'm glad I have teeth and don't have to eat sand. It was awful trying to eat when I didn't have my front teeth!"

"You looked pretty awful, too!" teased Annie.

Eliza's face clouded up. "You're mean, Annie Van Lew!"

"That's enough, girls." Aunt Elizabeth's voice held a hint of sternness. "She's only teasing you, Eliza. Don't be a crybaby when someone's funning you. You'll just have to learn to tease back. Now let's tell some stories. I'll start one, and when I stop Annie will carry it on, and when she stops Eliza will be next, then my turn again. We can get some strange stories that way!"

The rest of the trip home passed pleasantly, and it was just beginning to get dark as they pulled up the 24th Street hill to the stable. Ben met them and led Chieftain quickly into the shelter of the building. Annie noticed that the black man seemed very excited and nervous about something.

"Miss Lizzie, they was here again," he said as he unhitched the wagon. "The soldiers was nosin' all around again. I told them we didn't have no more horses. I told them they done got 'em all the last time they was here, but I don't think they b'lieved me. We was just lucky again that Chieftain weren't here. We gonna lose this horse too it we ain't careful!"

"Thank you, Ben. You did well." Aunt Elizabeth looked a little worried, Annie thought. It wasn't surprising. The horse was their only means of getting food from the farm. She looked in the back of the wagon. Nobody could have walked from the farm carrying even a small part of the load they had there. What if they didn't have all that food? Maybe they'd be like the starving people in Richmond that Dorcas talked about.

"When Chieftain's been fed you can start unloading the wagon, Ben," Aunt Elizabeth said. "And don't worry. I'll think of some way to save him if they come back. We should have some warning if they're in the neighborhood. Come on girls — into the house. Cook will have left a bite of supper for us."

Annie realized how hungry she was. It had been a long time since their picnic by the river, and even Mary's cookies and milk seemed far in the past.

Eliza almost fell asleep before they'd finished their pea soup and baking powder biscuits. She made no protest when Auntie carried her upstairs and tucked her in. Annie trailed behind them, unusually thankful for her nice warm supper.

It wasn't until after she'd hung up her clothes and was climbing into her big, four-poster bed that she remembered about the eggshell. Auntie hadn't answered her questions at all. She still didn't know who would have emptied the shell, and why it had been put in the basket with all the real eggs.

──Chapter 7

Annie awoke to the sound of heavy rain battering the window panes and a strong northeast wind swirling down the chimneys. She snuggled down deeper under her patchwork quilt. She hoped Chieftain was warm and dry in his stall, and that all the farm animals were comfortable in the barn. This was a day for all creatures to enjoy staying indoors.

She heard Eliza thumping down the stairs for breakfast, singing cheerily, if a bit off-key. Somewhere a door slammed. Reluctantly she decided it was time to get up.

After breakfast, when she came back upstairs to the library for her schoolwork, Aunt Elizabeth was waiting.

"Annie, what happened to you yesterday? This arithmetic paper is the worst I've seen in a long time. You only had two problems right! I know you understand the work, so this had to be just carelessness. That's not like you."

Annie looked at the toes of her shoes and shuffled her feet. She was remembering that she had decided not to check her work.

"I'm sorry, Auntie," she mumbled. "I guess I was just in too much of a hurry."

"Well, you can make up for it today. I expect you to do this work over correctly before you start on today's lessons. I've told Eliza to do her work down in the dining room so you won't be distracted. Then when you're finished, I want you to write a short essay on why carelessness does not pay. One page will do. You will stay here in the library till dinner time, so you'll have plenty of time to do a good job."

"Yes, Auntie." Annie grinned up at her. "I don't think I want to go out and play today anyway!"

Aunt Elizabeth laughed and gave her a hug. "Take your time and you'll do fine," she said as she left the room. "I'll close this door so no one will bother you."

Alone in the room Annie sat at the big table facing the fireplace. A cheery fire crackled and sent out comfortable tongues of warmth. She was not unhappy with Aunt Elizabeth's discipline. Sometimes she liked being quiet and by herself. The room was cozy, and the reflected firelight danced gracefully on the polished mahogany chairs. She picked up her pencil and went to work.

When she finally finished her essay, she glanced up at the mantle clock. She was surprised at how quickly she'd finished all her tasks. Even after checking everything over twice, there was still quite a bit of time left before dinner. She stood up and stretched, then wandered over to the windows that looked out over the porch and rear gardens. It was still raining steadily, and the sky was dark and gloomy.

She walked back to the fireplace and kicked at a glowing log. It broke, sending a cascade of sparks up the chimney. She took another log from the nearby basket, added it to the smouldering coals, and watched until the flames caught it.

As she turned away, the lion's head attracted her attention. It was hard to believe she'd ever seen it any way but perched solidly on top of its column. Uncertainly she reached out toward it. and gave the head a firm twist. It probably wouldn't really turn. But it did. There behind it was the space she'd seen. And, as before, there was something in it.

This time, alone in the closed room, Annie didn't hesitate. She pulled out the paper and took it back to the table. There she unfolded it and spread it out in front of her. Then she stared at it in bewilderment. She wasn't sure just what she'd expected, but it wasn't this — a series of numbers that were broken up into groups.

"I thought there'd be words on the paper — something to read," she said to herself. "This looks like arithmetic — like these numbers are just waiting for somebody to add them all up. But why would anyone want to? There's nothing to tell you if they mean dollars or apples or how many horses and cows the army has stolen!"

She looked thoughtfully at the rows of numbers. They were in groups of five, arranged in five columns of three groups each, with one extra group at the end. Maybe she would be able to figure it out later. A quick look at the clock told her it was getting close to dinner.

I don't know why these numbers were hidden under the lion's head, she thought, but I'd better put the paper back. It must be important to somebody, and I could get in real trouble it I kept it! But that doesn't mean I can't copy them!

Quickly she got pencil and paper and copied the numbers. She put the original back in its hiding place and returned the lion's head to its usual position. Curiously she studied her copy.

51111	15341	41115	35124	53515
15411	24116	16511	61246	11165
36616	34536	51514	15361	54436
30000				

She shook her head as she folded up her copy and tucked it in her apron pocket. It has to mean something, she thought on her way down to dinner. But I think it's going to take me a long time to figure it out!

——Chapter 8

Annie spent most of the afternoon in her room, puzzling over the series of numbers she'd found. No matter what she tried, no matter how she worked with them, nothing seemed to make any sense. Finally she gave up and decided she'd never understand them until she knew what they stood for, and why they were hidden in the lion's head. She folded the paper into a small square and poked it into the toe of one of her best Sunday shoes for safekeeping.

The rain continued for three more days. At first Annie enjoyed being inside and cozy. She practiced her music on the big rosewood piano in the parlor. She dug out a sampler she'd started when she was younger, and did some embroidery, but she didn't really enjoy it, and soon gave it up.

She read to Eliza, and played countless games of checkers with her. She even helped her rearrange the furniture in the doll's house and make new curtains for the little windows. They tried to make new clothes for Eliza's doll, but Annie hated sewing, and Eliza wasn't very good at it, so the project was not a success.

Even Dorcas wasn't much fun anymore. The black maid seemed to have her mind on something else and paid only slight attention to Annie.

On Sunday they went to St. John's Church, but even that didn't lift her spirits. The Van Lews sloshed across the street in a downpour and sat damp and uncomfortable all through the service. Aunt Elizabeth wore her long cape and ugly brown bonnet, and all three of them had heavy muddy boots on. Annie could hear people around them whispering to each other about Aunt Elizabeth. She'd heard them before, and she knew what they probably were saying.

"There's Crazy Betty Van Lew! She's pro-Union, you know!"

"She absolutely refused to sew shirts for our fine Confederate boys!"

"She takes food to those awful men in Libby prison! When our own people are starving!"

"They shouldn't allow people like that in our church. Why, she's not even a true Virginian! Her father came from Long Island, and her mother from Philadelphia!"

"Of course, she's tetched in the head. Those poor little girls shouldn't be allowed to stay with her!"

Annie shot an angry glance behind her. She knew Aunt Elizabeth was smart and loving and kind — there was nothing crazy about her at all. But why did she have to do such strange things? She wore such ugly clothes when she went out, and walked with those funny little sideways steps, and sang off-key in that dreadful high squeaky voice. It was sort of her own fault that people said such nasty things about her. Auntie didn't seem to mind, and sometimes it seemed to amuse her. But it wouldn't be funny if someone decided that Annie and Eliza couldn't live with her anymore. Where would they go then? She moved closer to Aunt Eiizabeth in the pew and reached out to catch her hand tightly, receiving a gentle squeeze in return.

A boy sitting behind them gave one of Annie's ringlets a painful tug. She gritted her teeth and stared straight ahead. If Auntie could ignore mean people, so could she! She wouldn't give him the satisfaction of knowing it hurt.

But she grinned with quiet delight when she heard his mother give him a smack and heard his muffled howl of protest. She wished they didn't have to go to church and be with people who didn't want them around. She was glad she had lessons at home instead of going to school. School with boys like that would be awful! But she did wish she had a girl friend. It was lonely, with only Eliza to play with.

When the long service was over, they went straight home and changed into dry clothing. Annie felt much better after dinner. They'd had her favorite fried ham with red-eye gravy, and she sort of liked the green beans and boiled potatoes. But the real treat was the dessert of hot biscuits and honey. She wished everyone could have such a good meal.

After dinner, Eliza said she was going to play with her doll's house, and Aunt Elizabeth went up to the library to write some letters. Annie drifted about aimlessly, not sure what she wanted to do.

After fingering the piano keys idly for a few minutes she wandered up to her room, pulled the paper with its mysterious numbers from its hiding place, and stared at it. Then she tucked it away again. It didn't mean any more now than when she'd first copied it.

"I'm lonely," she said to herself. "I wish there was someone to do something with — something that I like to do." She stood at the window, staring out at the rain. "I hate this weather!"

Her thoughts wandered to the soldiers camped out in the rain. At least she was warm and dry and well fed. They only had tents for shelter, and never enough food. And what about the black people in the city, who, now that they were free, didn't have homes to go to or jobs to earn money. She wondered if Papa had enough to eat.

Suddenly Annie realized that she didn't want to be alone anymore. She crossed the hall to the library and padded over the thick rug to stand near Aunt Elizabeth's desk.

"Will it bother you if I stay in here, Auntie?" she asked. "I thought I'd see if I can find something to read."

"Go ahead, honey. There's lots of books to choose from."

Annie roamed quietly about, taking down one book here, another there, then returning them to their places. Then, over in a dark corner of the room, she found several history books that looked interesting. She chose a biography of George Washington, curled up in a big chair near a window, and started reading. The room was quiet except for the scratching of Aunt Elizabeth's pen and the ticking of the mantle clock.

When Annie looked up, daylight had faded, and Aunt Elizabeth had gone. She moved over to sit by the lamp on her aunt's desk, hoping to finish the chapter before supper. As she turned a page, she noticed that the lamplight seemed to be shining through tiny holes in the paper. Someone had punched holes in the paper with something sharp — a pin, maybe. Annie could feel the little bumps when she ran her finger over the page. She looked closer, and discovered another surprise — the holes had been punched through letters only, not blank spaces. Curiously she picked up a pencil and paper and began to copy down the letters that had holes in them.

CONFEDERATE

Excitement swept through her. The letters were spelling out words — <u>real</u> words that she could read! This wasn't like that jumble of numbers she'd found earlier. This made sense. But who had done it, and why?

She copied down the letters with punched holes in them, and her excitement grew as each word became clear. This was a real message — a message with meaning! When she could find no more tiny holes, she leaned back to read what she had written.

CONFEDERATE GENERAL EARLY ADVANCING
ON WASHINGTON FROM SHENANDOAH VALLEY

She dropped the paper back on the desk and sighed in disappointment. This was a very old secret message. I hoped it would be something important, she thought, but this had to have been done a long time ago. General Jubal Early moved toward Washington way last summer. General Sherman and the Union troops beat him thoroughly in the fall.

She stood up and stretched. Even if the message wasn't new, it was still a mystery who had sent it, and who had received it, and why it was in a book in the Van Lew library.

"I think I'll save this anyway," she said to herself. "Something strange seems to be going on, and I wish I knew what it was. Maybe I'll be able to figure it out later."

She blew out the lamp on the desk, crossed the hall to her bedroom, and hid this message in her shoe with the other one from the lion's head. As she went downstairs to supper, she wondered if there was any connection between the two messages, and if she'd ever understand what it was.

──Chapter 9

The next day was a beautiful, sunny one, and as soon as lessons were over, Annie and Eliza raced outdoors. It felt so good to run up and down the garden paths after being indoors for so long! They stopped at the bottom of the yard to catch their breaths, and stood watching the activity on Main Street below them. As usual, it was noisy and crowded with all sorts of people, some moving hurriedly on unknown errands, others lounging against trees and lampposts, still others scurrying off to disappear between buildings. Hordes of boys chased after wagons, and soldiers tramped past. The din was constant, blending with the occasional rumble of distant gunfire.

Eliza tugged at Annie's sleeve. "Look! Isn't that Auntie and Dorcas down there?"

Annie looked where she was pointing. Sure enough, there was Aunt Elizabeth bobbing along through the crowd, basket on her arm, the ugly old bonnet hiding her face. Dorcas was following her with another basket, and several boys were circling around them, pointing and laughing. Annie could almost hear their chant of "Crazy Bett!"

"They're taking food to the prison, I guess," she said. "This is the first good weather we've had since we brought the food from the farm."

"Why does Auntie have to take the prisoners food? Don't the soldiers who captured them have to feed them?"

"They're supposed to. But the army doesn't have enough food even for themselves. Dorcas told me that some of the prisoners get boxes of things from their families up north. They come up the river on barges, but they get broken into and stuff gets stolen before the prisoners ever get them."

"That's mean! It's not right to steal other people's things!" Eliza's voice was indignant.

"You and I know that, but maybe the thieves don't. And anyway, Dorcas says you never know what people will do if they're cold enough and hungry enough!"

"Just the same, it's mean. I'm glad Auntie shares our food with the prisoners. It's nicer than stealing!"

They watched until Aunt Elizabeth and Dorcas disappeared from sight, then they ran back up the hill to visit Chieftain in the stable and the kittens in the carriage house. The kittens were getting bigger and were playfully chasing each other, stumbling all over their own over-sized feet. Eliza was enchanted with them, but Annie soon left, looking for something more interesting to do.

Delicious smells drew her to the kitchen house. Like most large southern homes, the Van Lew mansion did not have a kitchen in the main house. The cooking was done in a separate building. This kept the big house cooler in summer, free of cooking odors, and lessened the danger of fire. Slaves or servants carried the food to the dining room and served the family meals there. Annie liked the kitchen at the farm, but had never been in the kitchen at her Grace Street home.

That smells like fresh gingerbread, she thought. Maybe I can get some, and maybe Cook will show me how to make it.

She stood just inside the doorway, watching Cook and her helper bustle about. A pan of gingerbread, fresh from the oven, steamed on the big table in the middle of the room. Cook was wiping up some spills with a damp cloth when she looked up and saw Annie. A look of dismay spread over her round, black face.

"Miss Annie! You get out of here! This ain't no place for a lady!" As if to emphasize her words, she flung her damp cloth in Annie's direction. Annie turned and fled.

Safely outside, Annie wasn't sure whether to be angry or amused. She knew most wealthy southern women wouldn't think of doing their own cooking as long as there was someone to do it for them. But she also knew she wasn't a "lady" yet, just a little girl curious about how to make gingerbread. Besides, she'd have to learn about cooking and kitchens someday so she could manage her own home when she grew up. Maybe Aunt Elizabeth would ask Cook to teach Annie and Eliza someday. It would be fun to learn something more interesting than arithmetic!

—Chapter 10

Annie sat on the floor of the rear porch of her home, leaning against one of the six tall pillars that rose above the second floor windows to the roof. Her feet dangled over the edge while she watched the lively scene on the river below. Boats and barges of all sizes and shapes skittered about in all directions like busy water-bugs. She wondered if the war would ever end, so Papa could come home and open up his hardware store again, and the people could all go home and raise their own food on their own farms, so they could have enough to eat.

She was startled out of her daydreaming by Aunt Elizabeth's voice. "Annie, I need your help. Come quickly!"

"What is it?" Auntie sounded more anxious than usual. Annie scrambled to her feet and ran into the house.

"The soldiers are up on Church Hill looking for horses again. They're over on Broad Street now. We have to get Chieftain to a safe place!"

Oh no! We can't lose him now, Annie thought, beginning to shake a little. We must save him! But how? "What shall I do, Auntie?" she asked with a slight tremble in her voice.

"Go to the stable, put a halter on him, and bring him into the house by the back basement door. Hurry, now!"

Annie stared at her. "In the house?"

"You heard me! Go!"

As Annie ran to the stable she passed Ben, carrying a large bag of straw on his shoulder. He was headed toward the house. I must be dreaming, she thought. This can't be real. Horses don't go into houses!

She led Chieftain out of his stall and started back across the yard. She passed Ben again on his way back to the stable.

"Good girl, Miss Annie! Get him inside. I got to get more straw." He hurried on.

Aunt Elizabeth met her at the door under the big porch where Annie had been sitting so peacefully just a few minutes ago.

"Take him up to the library. Eliza will help if you need her." Auntie sped off around the corner of the house, leaving Annie and Chieftain in the doorway.

"I don't believe I'm really doing this!" she said aloud to herself as she headed toward the stairs, followed by the big brown horse. She started up, tugging at the halter rope. Chieftain followed her meekly, stepping as surely as if this were something he did every day.

Eliza was waiting in the front hall of the first floor. "Can I help, Annie? Let me help!"

"Get up front here with me so we can both pull if we have to. I don't know if he's going to like these big wide stairs with the open railing."

Up they went, Chieftain's footsteps muffled by the thick carpeting. Annie decided it was lucky the stairs were covered. Horseshoes could have made scars on the hardwood finish and might have given away their secret.

In the library Ben had spread straw along the side of the room that was away from the windows. Annie led Chieftain over there and tethered him to a leg of the big heavy table where they did their schoolwork. She smoothed his nose lovingly, and leaned her head against his neck.

"You're a good horse, Chieftain," she whispered to him. "You be nice and quiet now. We don't want those Confederate soldiers to get you!" She shivered a little at the thought of Chieftain as a Confederate horse. It would be dreadful for him to have to pull a heavy cannon, or be ridden wildly into a battle. He would surely be hungry, maybe beaten. He might even be killed!

Ben and Aunt Elizabeth came into the room, he with more straw, and she carrying a bucket of water and a nosebag of food.

"All right, girls. Thank you. You did a fine job. Now I want you both to go outdoors. Go down to the bottom of the garden and play there until I send Dorcas to get you. Stay out of sight if you see any soldiers. I don't want them to start asking you questions you might not want to answer."

Annie wished she could stay and see what happened when the soldiers came. But she knew Auntie was right. Annie might be able to keep the secret, no matter what they asked her, but she wasn't so sure about Eliza. She was still young enough to blurt out things by mistake and be sorry afterwards.

Time seemed to drag as Annie and Eliza hovered around the area of the gazebo. No soldiers came near there, and Annie ran out of ideas of quiet games for them to play. She wished she'd brought a book they could have read. It was a dull afternoon.

It was almost dark when Dorcas came for them, and Annie was beginning to feel hungry.

"What happened, Dorcas? Did the soldiers come? Is Chieftain safe? Is he still in the house? Is supper ready?" Her questions came tumbling out like apples spilling from a basket.

"Slow down, Miss Annie! One question at a time, please!" Dorcas laughed. "Chieftain is fine. And yes, he's still in the house. And supper is almost ready."

Eliza looked puzzled. "Is he going to stay there? Are the soldiers coming back?"

"We hope not! Chieftain is still in the house because he won't come out! He won't walk down the stairs."

Annie was astonished. "Why, I didn't have any trouble at all making him walk upstairs!"

"Up and down are two different things, Miss Annie. Down is harder for a horse. Stairs ain't natural for him in either case."

"How will we ever get him out, Dorcas?" Eliza asked.

"Miss Lizzie and Ben are right smart about horses. She sent him to get some old boards from the carriage house, and they're making a ramp for him to use. He'll go down a hill when he won't use steps."

Annie started running. "Hurry! I want to see, before he's all the way down!"

They arrived in time to see Chieftain inching cautiously down the ramp laid over the wide front stairs. Annie held him while they moved the boards to the basement steps for the next part of his journey. She nuzzled him lovingly. "Good boy, Chieftain! Good boy! You're safe now!" She loved him so much!

At supper Aunt Elizabeth told them all about the soldiers' visit. They had searched every one of the outbuildings, even the kitchen, to Cook's great annoyance, and had finally come into the house. She had served them tea in the parlor, with some of the left-over gingerbread, and they had finally left, convinced that the Van Lews had no more horses. They had taken the live chickens, though. "But I can't begrudge them that," she added. "They were hungry."

"I hope they don't come back," Annie said. She wished this terrible war would end and everybody would go home and be happy and stop stealing. She didn't like worrying about Papa and Chieftain and hungry, homeless people.

"So do I," Auntie agreed. "But we won't take any chances. Tomorrow I'll take Chieftain to the farm for Matt to guard. There are many more hiding places there. We couldn't pull this trick again safely. We were lucky he didn't stamp or neigh while they were in the house." She smiled a little. "He's a very good and loyal Union horse!"

—Chapter 11

"May I go with you to the farm, Auntie?" asked Annie as they sat at breakfast.

"Not today, honey." Aunt Elizabeth pushed back her chair and stood up. "I'm not going to be taking the wagon." She carried her empty dishes to the tray on the sideboard, then turned to leave the dining room. "We want to get Chieftain away from here as quickly as possible, and it will be much safer and faster if I ride him."

"But how will you get back?" asked Eliza. "It's a long way to walk!"

Aunt Elizabeth stopped in the doorway and laughed. "I've walked that far lots of times, Eliza, but not today. I'm going to make a trade with Matt. We'll give him Chieftain to take care of, and he'll give us Spook to use here. I'll ride him home."

Annie and Eliza looked at each other and giggled. They could just imagine how funny Auntie would look riding the old, sway-backed grey mule.

"I know I'll look pretty strange," Aunt Elizabeth said. "But Spook is still a useful animal, both for riding and pulling the wagon. He just isn't a very handsome beast. I doubt if even the army would think him worth stealing, but he'll do everything we need of him. Don't wait for me if I'm not back by dinner time. I may spend some time looking over things at the farm with Matt." She left the room, and they could hear her saying something to someone in the front hallway, but her voice was muffled and Annie could not understand her words.

Annie decided she would practice her music before she did her schoolwork, and went directly into the front parlor as soon as she finished eating. From where she sat at the piano she could see out onto Grace Street toward 23rd Street, almost as far as the corner. To her surprise, there went Aunt Elizabeth's bonnet and cloak, just disappearing beyond her view. Jumping up she went closer to the window to see better.

She knew it couldn't be Aunt Elizabeth. Her aunt was headed in the other direction on horseback and was wearing her riding clothes. It must be Dorcas again! But why? It was broad daylight, so she didn't have to worry about thieves stealing her good coat like she'd said the other time Annie had seen her in Auntie's clothes.

As Annie stood there, frowning thoughtfully, she saw a man slip out from behind some shrubbery across the street and head after the hurrying maid. Was he following Dorcas? He was small, with a big, bushy beard. He wore a black frock coat and a bowler hat. He did not look at all like the usual person one saw on the streets of Church Hill on a sunny weekday morning.

Annie was a little worried now. Where was Dorcas going, and why was the man following her? She wished Aunt Elizabeth were here. For a moment Annie hesitated, then she made a decision. If Dorcas was going to be in trouble or danger from the man following her, someone should know about it. Dorcas might need help! She thought about getting Ben, then realized that by the time she found him and he stopped whatever he was doing, Dorcas and her shadower would have disappeared. There was only one thing to do. Running quickly to the basement, she grabbed her coat and dashed out onto the street. The man was just past the corner, with Dorcas striding along half a block ahead of him.

Staying as close to the fence as possible, away from the curb, Annie followed the two along the brick walk. She hoped the man wouldn't turn around and see her, but he seemed only to be interested in Dorcas ahead of him and not concerned about who might be behind him.

A few blocks farther along, Annie saw Dorcas turn south toward the river. After two blocks she turned west again on Main Street. She seemed to be heading toward Capitol Square. Up ahead loomed the big State House building.

"I hope she doesn't go on too much longer," Annie said to herself. "I don't want to get much farther away from home. It's kind of scary, and nobody knows where I am. Maybe I'd better turn around."

Just then, Dorcas stopped in front of a small shop. She hesitated a moment, then disappeared inside. The man behind her slowed his steps, then stopped and leaned against a nearby building, as if he were interested in nothing in particular. Annie stopped too. She recognized the shop Dorcas had entered as the dressmaker's. She'd been there herself with Auntie.

There was nothing between her and the man but empty sidewalk, not even the usual crowd of hurrying people, and no place for her to hide if he turned around. What would he think or do if he saw her? Would he know that she'd been following him? She moved as close to the building as she could, and wished she could become invisible.

The man shifted his position a little, and Annie held her breath until he settled against the building again. She guessed he hadn't noticed her, or maybe he didn't care that she was there. She wished that Dorcas would come out of the shop. But what would she do if Dorcas went farther into town and the man still followed her? How long and how far did she dare to trail after them?

In a few minutes Dorcas came back out onto the street and turned toward home. There was no way Annie could avoid being seen. As she stood there, waiting for Dorcas to join her, she was surprised to hear the man utter a curse, then scurry off down a side street toward the river. Dorcas seemed to pay no attention to him, but came hurrying toward Annie, a frown on her usually cheerful dark face.

"Miss Annie! What in the world are you doing here? You know better than to be out alone on the streets these days! It's foolish and dangerous, and Miss Lizzie'd have your hide if she knew!"

"Don't tell, Dorcas, please!" Annie pleaded. "I was only trying to help you!"

"Help me? How you gonna help me by wanderin' around Richmond alone? Miss Lizzie'd skin me alive if something happened to you!" Dorcas sounded both angry and frightened. Annie winced a little as she felt Dorcas' strong fingers on her arm as she was hurried along.

"That man was following you. I wanted to be able to get help if he hurt you. He was hiding in the bushes across the street and followed you all the way from home!" Annie's voice was shaky, and she knew her chin trembled. She hated it when people were angry at her, even when she knew she deserved it.

"Well, he didn't bother me, and he's gone on his way to someplace else. Step along now! We'll get you home before Miss Lizzie gets back, and I'll think about what to tell her. She really ought to know you've done such a foolish thing! This is wartime, Miss Annie, and Richmond is right in the middle of it!" Dorcas was very serious, and Annie knew in her own heart that she was right.

She hurried her words. "I'm sorry, Dorcas. I guess I just didn't think. Will you promise not to tell if I promise not to leave the yard alone again?"

Dorcas spoke sharply. "I won't bargain with you, Miss Annie. This is too serious a matter for bargains. We'll see. When we get home you get straight to your schoolwork, and don't give me any more trouble. Just think a little bit about what might have happened."

Back home, Annie sat in the quiet library and did her work. When she'd finished her lessons, she continued to sit there for a while, thinking very hard. Then she made a decision and stood up. She was feeling a little better already. When Auntie came home, she'd tell her what happened herself. Aunt Elizabeth should know, not just because Annie had done something foolish and dangerous, but because she should know about the man following Dorcas. Auntie was strict but fair, but Annie dreaded telling her. It wasn't going to be easy!

──Chapter 12

Aunt Elizabeth was not home in time for dinner. Annie ate very little. She found it hard to swallow, and nothing tasted very good. She pushed her food around on her plate for a while, then gave up trying to eat and went outdoors. Maybe she'd feel better in the fresh air.

Eliza asked her to play with her, but Annie was cross and snappish, and Eliza ended up running away in tears. That made Annie feel even worse. Eliza wasn't much fun to play with because she was three years younger, but there wasn't anybody else. They had only each other.

"I hate it that no one is allowed to be friends with us," Annie muttered to herself as she wandered down through the gardens, kicking at the gravel on the path. "And Aunt Elizabeth doesn't have any friends either. I wonder if she's as lonely as I am. Probably not, or she wouldn't act so strange and make people think she's crazy. I wonder why she does that? I should think she'd <u>want</u> people to like her. I do."

She turned around and started back up through the yard, not sure where she was going or what she was going to do when she arrived there.

I wish Auntie would get home, she thought. I want to get this over with and take my punishment. It's worse thinking about it than being punished. She stopped in at the stable and looked sadly at Chieftain's empty stall. She missed him already. Spook was a nice mule, and she wouldn't mind having him around, but he wasn't the same as the big brown horse. She hoped Chieftain would be safe at the farm. He'd always be her favorite, no matter where he was.

As she left the stable she was startled to hear someone call her name.

"Miss Annie! Miss Annie! Over here!"

She turned toward the voice. Mary stood in the shadow of a tree, near the corner of the carriage house.

Annie ran to her eagerly. "Mary! How wonderful to see you! But what are you doing here? I thought Mrs. Davis wouldn't let you come to our house!"

Mary grabbed her arm and pulled her quickly into the shelter of the empty carriage house. "She doesn't know. She sent me on an errand and I ran all the way here. I don't have much time. I must see Miss Lizzie. Will you tell her I'm here?"

"Auntie isn't home. She's gone to the farm. I don't know when she'll be back."

"Dorcas, then. Tell Dorcas!" Mary was panting and she seemed quite nervous.

"I don't know where she is," Annie said. "I haven't seen her since this morning. Want me to look for her?"

Mary looked dismayed. "I don't have that much time. I have to get back before Mrs. Davis wonders why I've been gone so long!"

"I'm here," Annie said. "Can I help?"

"I don't know," said Mary slowly. "Maybe. Can I trust you to give Miss Lizzie a message as soon as she gets back?"

"Of course!" Annie wasn't sure whether to feel insulted or not. "If I say I'll do something, I do it."

What could be so important, she wondered, that Mary would run all the way over here to tell Aunt Elizabeth about it?

"Well, then, get some paper and a pencil quickly. I'll wait right here."

Annie sped into the house, charged up the stairs to the library, grabbed a pencil and paper from her school things and dashed back to the carriage house.

"Here," she gasped.

Mary took the paper and wrote rapidly for a minute. Then she folded the sheet twice and gave it to Annie. "Please see Miss Lizzie gets this as soon as you can. It's important."

"I promise," said Annie. "But I didn't know you could write, Mary. That must mean you can read, too!"

"Yes. When Miss Lizzie set us free, she made my father her farm manager. She taught him to do accounts and things, and she sent me north to be educated in a real school in Philadelphia. I can probably read and write as well as you can, Miss Annie. Maybe better. Now I have to hurry, or Mrs. Davis will get after me for dawdling!"

Annie watched Mary's tall figure hurry up the 24th Street hill and disappear around the corner onto Broad Street.

I wonder what's so important for Auntie to know, she thought. What could Mary possibly have to say to her that couldn't wait?

She looked at the paper in her hand, and turned it over once or twice. It seemed to be burning her fingers. Finally, she said to herself, "I didn't promise not to read it. Only to make sure Auntie gets it as soon as possible." She hesitated another moment, then unfolded the paper.

"Mrs. Davis selling furniture and making plans to leave with children. Has little hope of saving Richmond and feels war is lost."

Annie read the words a second time. If this is true, she thought solemnly, things are indeed very bad for the Confederacy. Auntie will be glad to know this.

She walked slowly into the house and upstairs to her room. She pulled her good shoes from the wardrobe and dug out the hidden papers. She sat on the edge of her bed and stared at the three messages. One made no sense, one was old, and Mary's didn't really seem to be very urgent or important. But they must all be connected.

At least I won't have to copy this one, she thought. I won't have any trouble remembering it.

"Now I'll probably never get to know Maggie Davis, even after the war is over," she said a little sadly. "I wish she could have been my friend. She looks as if we would have liked each other."

She wondered what would happen if Richmond was lost by the Confederates. Would there by danger to her home and family? Would Yankee soldiers come stealing and burning? Would they be safe because Auntie loved the Union? She shuddered a little with the fears that were buzzing around in her mind like angry bees. She'd best try to think of other things, even about her coming punishment.

She tucked the papers back into her shoe and tossed it back into the wardrobe. She put the message from Mary into her apron pocket, and drifted downstairs and out onto the big rear porch.

"I'll just sit here and watch the boats and wait for Auntie," she said to herself, dropping down on the edge and leaning against a pillar. "She and I will have a lot to talk about."

——Chapter 13

Aunt Elizabeth did not arrive home until late afternoon. Annie saw her ride up the hill from Main Street and turn into the stable. In spite of her uneasiness and worry about facing her aunt with the story of the morning's activities, Annie couldn't help but giggle. Auntie looked just as peculiar riding old Spook as she and Eliza had imagined.

Aunt Elizabeth was not a large woman, but Spook was quite a small mule. Either Spook was too small for Auntie, or she was too big for him! I'd fit him better than Auntie does, Annie thought. Maybe I can ride him sometimes.

She started toward the stable, then stopped. "I don't think I want to talk to Auntie right now," she said to herself. "I need more time to build up my courage!"

But putting off talking to Auntie wasn't helping, and she'd promised Mary to deliver the message as soon as possible. She took a deep breath and marched into the house, trying not to shake as she climbed the stairs. Maybe Mary's message is so important Auntie won't take the time to listen to my confession, she hoped. Maybe Auntie will want to tell someone else about it right away. Somebody else who's loyal to the Union. Auntie has said there are others. Maybe ... Maybe ... Annie sighed. All the maybes in the world wouldn't change the fact that sometime she was going to have to face Aunt Elizabeth and take her medicine. She might as well get it over with.

Aunt Elizabeth was seated at her desk in the library, entering figures in an account book.

"Auntie ..."

"Why, hello Annie. I didn't hear you come in. You'll be glad to know that Chieftain is safely in Matt's care, and Ben is getting Spook all settled in his new home."

"Here." Annie held out the paper message. "Mary brought this over today. I said I'd give it to you."

She saw the frown on Auntie's face as she took the paper and glanced at it quickly.

"What's wrong, Annie? You aren't acting like yourself at all! Did you read this? Are you upset because of what this says?"

Annie could feel her eyes fill with tears. They started to run down her cheeks like raindrops on a windowpane, and she wished she had a handkerchief to mop them up.

"Oh, Auntie," she sniffled. "I did read it — Mary didn't say not to. But that's not the trouble!"

Between gulps and snuffles she poured out the tale of the morning's adventure. Her throat ached and her eyes stung, and she felt very much alone as she stood facing Aunt Elizabeth. Through her tears she could see that the expression on Auntie's face was serious, but calm. She didn't seem to be excited or distressed by Annie's story, and she listened very carefully and thoughtfully.

At last Annie came to the end. "Oh, Auntie! I'm so sorry. I didn't mean to disobey you about going out alone. I was just worried about Dorcas!"

To her relief, Aunt Elizabeth smiled at her. "Come here, honey. Into my lap!"

Annie rushed behind the desk and into the welcoming arms that squeezed her till she could hardly breathe.

"There now. Here's a handkerchief for those tears." Auntie's loving, comforting voice flowed around her like a fire's welcome warmth on a winter day. She gulped once or twice more, swallowed hard, and settled herself more comfortably in Auntie's soft lap.

"Let's talk a little," Aunt Elizabeth said. "I think you were a very brave girl to follow Dorcas and the man this morning. I'm proud of you for caring enough about her to worry, and for trying to help when you thought she might be in danger. I think you deserve to know what it was all about."

Annie snuggled closer, and leaned her cheek against Aunt Elizabeth's shoulder. "I'm almost too big for your lap," she said, "even if I haven't grown much lately."

"But not too big for loving and cuddling." Annie could hear a smile in Auntie's voice, even if she couldn't see her face. "This morning, after breakfast, I told Dorcas to put on my cape and bonnet and go to the dressmaker's shop. I knew the man was there in the bushes across the street. He's been there for two days now."

"But why?"

"He's a detective, and I think he's been following me. I saw him behind us in the crowd the last time Dorcas and I went to the prison, and other times, too, I think. I thought today would be a good chance to find out, because he wouldn't know I was taking Chieftain to the farm. If he thought I was going to town and followed Dorcas, then I'd know I was right." She laughed a little. "From what you say, he must have been mighty surprised when Dorcas came out of the shop and he saw her dark face instead of my white one!"

Annie laughed too, remembering the man's startled expression, then took another deep breath. "But Auntie. I know it was wrong of me to leave the yard alone, with no one knowing where I was. I won't ever do it again, I promise!" She trembled a little as she wondered what her punishment would be.

Auntie gave her a quick hug. "You've been worrying about this all day, haven't you?"

Annie nodded, still feeling the choking of tears in her throat.

"I think perhaps that's punishment enough," Auntie said gently. "So we won't say any more about it."

Annie's thoughts went back to Mary's message. "Auntie, if Mrs. Davis is right, maybe the war will be over soon and it'll be safe to walk around in Richmond. All the soldiers and sailors and farmers and prisoners will go home, and all the freed slaves will find work and a place to live."

"Maybe." Aunt Elizabeth's voice didn't sound too sure. "Anyway, I do have to let some other people know about this message, people who love the Union and are making plans for handling affairs when the fighting stops. I'll go see Ben and have him deliver this to one of them, so the word will spread. Hop up, now, and go wash that teary face!"

As Annie watched Aunt Elizabeth leave the library, she began to wonder. Why in the world would a detective be following Auntie? What did detectives do, anyway? She knew they tried to find missing people — but Auntie wasn't missing. She'd heard they caught murderers — but Auntie certainly had never killed anyone! Some people thought she was crazy, but why would anyone waste money paying a detective to follow a crazy lady when the price of food was so high? Annie sighed. She wondered if any of this would ever make sense to her.

—Chapter 14

Annie lay in her big four-poster bed and stared up at the fringed canopy over her head. Her room was dark because there was no moonlight at all. The next full moon and Easter were still more than two weeks away. But her eyes were accustomed to the dim light, and she was so comfortably familiar with her room that she didn't need much light to see where things were.

It was long past her bedtime, but she wasn't the least bit sleepy. The house was quiet. Outside she could hear the distant noises of the city which never seemed to sleep, but the far-away gunfire from the siege of Petersburg had stopped, at least for a little while. In a tree near the house a night bird was calling, and she could hear another answering it from down at the other end of the garden.

Won't it be wonderful when this war is over, she thought. When everything is peaceful and quiet like this, even the city, because all the noisy, disturbing outsiders will have gone home. If Mrs. Davis is right, maybe it won't be long now.

66

A muffled thump over her head startled her from her drifting thoughts. She sat straight up in bed and stared intently at the canopy over her head. If only she could see through it and the ceiling above and discover what had made the unexpected sound! She was tense and unmoving. After a moment or two, when there was no further noise, she leaned back among her pillows, more wide-awake than ever.

What could have caused that thump? The third floor of the house was used only for storage. There were rooms there, and a built-in cupboard or two, but no one lived up there. She climbed out of bed and tiptoed to her door. She listened carefully, but couldn't hear any noise in the house at all. Of course Dorcas and Cook had rooms in the basement, so she wouldn't be able to hear them anyway. Ben slept in a cozy room in the stable, and Bessie, the laundress, came in on washing days from her home in the city. She, Eliza, and Auntie had rooms on the second floor. No one belonged up on the third floor, especially in the middle of the night! But something was up there — something that went "thump"!

She thought for a minute about going up there to see what — or who — was there, but decided against it. She had no way to light either her candle or her lamp. She always brought her lighted lamp up from the first floor when she went to bed. And anyway, moving around up there might very well wake up Auntie, and that didn't seem like a very good idea. Tomorrow morning would be time enough. She climbed back into bed and snuggled down.

She hated to admit it, even to herself, but she wasn't too anxious to go up those stairs in the dark, not knowing what she'd find when she reached the top. If someone was there who shouldn't be, it could be dangerous. She was curious, but not foolhardy! It was one thing to follow Dorcas and the detective on a bright, sunny morning. It was quite another to go up into a dark attic in the middle of the night to look for a noise!

While she lay there she tried to guess what could have caused the thump. Then she heard another funny sound. Only a few minutes had passed since she'd first heard the thump. Now there was a long, soft, scraping noise. Was something being dragged across the floor? I'm scared, she thought! I'm not afraid of dogs, or the dark, or thunderstorms, but I don't like noises in an empty room in the middle of the night! She felt very young and helpless and frightened. She burrowed down deeper in her bed, pulled the pillows over her head, and wondered how long it was till morning.

—Chapter 15

The bright light coming through her bedroom windows woke Annie after a long night broken by frightening dreams. Often she had awakened to lie alert and tense, waiting for a repetition of the noises over her head.

She had slept much later than usual, she realized, as she noticed how the light brightened a different part of the carpet from where it did most mornings. She hoped she wasn't too late for breakfast!

Alone in the dining room she gobbled the cold cornbread and buttermilk left waiting at her place, and thought about what she was going to do next. After putting her dishes on the tray on the sideboard, she went looking for Aunt Elizabeth.

No one seemed to be around. Perhaps this would be a good time to check the third floor. If something was wrong up there, Auntie should be told about it. As she climbed the narrow stairs from the second floor, she realized that her heart was pounding much faster than usual. Her hands felt clammy, and her legs seemed heavy. She had to use all her will power to keep going.

At the top of the stairs she stopped and listened. Silence. There wasn't any noise from the floors below, and none from outdoors. Of course the windows on this floor would all be closed, but she wished she could hear something familiar — a dog barking, or a bird singing. Even distant gunfire would be a welcome sound, reassuring in its commonplace, everyday thundering.

She drew a deep breath and started down the hallway, gaining courage with every step. There was nothing strange or out of place up here at all. The rooms were the same as they always were, some filled with unused furniture, some with boxes and trunks, some completely empty. There was one room arranged as an extra bedroom, and she knew this was where unexpected guests sometimes stayed in the old days before the war, but they never had guests anymore.

The hallway had several low bookcases along the wall, filled with old, dusty ledgers and account books, and near one end there was a small dresser that she knew held outgrown clothing. Everything seemed very ordinary.

She clattered back downstairs, ran outdoors into the bright sunshine, and breathed deeply of the warm spring air. It was refreshing after the stale, still atmosphere of the third floor. It felt so good to have that long, scary night behind her! And to know that everything was as it should be in the house. She certainly hoped it would stay that way. She didn't want another night like the last one!

As she skipped along the paths, she decided to go see Spook in the stable. The little mule must be lonely in his new home, and might welcome someone to pat his nose and give him some loving attention. To her surprise, his stall was empty, and there was no sign of Ben or the wagon. Where <u>was</u> everyone? She would even have been glad to see Eliza or the kittens, but Eliza was nowhere to be found, and the kittens had all left their box on some expedition of their own.

She plopped down on the grass near the stable door. "What am I going to do now?" she said aloud. "Auntie didn't even leave any lessons for me to do! And there's nobody around to talk to, not even Spook or the kittens!"

She felt a little sorry for herself until she heard footsteps coming along the path toward her. To her delight, it was Aunt Elizabeth. She was carrying two large baskets, and in spite of the warmth of the day, she was wearing her old cloak and bonnet. She smiled when she saw Annie, who scrambled to her feet as Auntie set the baskets down.

"There you are, Miss Sleepy-Head! I was wondering if you were going to sleep till noon!"

"I didn't sleep very well last night," said Annie, "so I guess I made up for it this morning."

"Are you sure you're feeling well?"

"I'm fine. I just had some bad dreams."

Aunt Elizabeth gave her a comforting hug. "Bad dreams can be very distressing. I've had some myself."

"Where is everybody?" asked Annie. "I can't even find Spook!"

"Spook and Ben have taken the wagon to the farm. Ben wants to be sure Chieftain is still all right, and we need some more food supplies. Since the soldiers took our chickens we haven't had any fresh meat, or eggs either."

"Where's Eliza?"

"She and Dorcas have gone into town to do some errands for me. You could have gone too, but you were sound asleep when I saw you last! How would you like to help me instead?" Aunt Elizabeth added the last part so quickly that Annie knew her disappointment must have shown on her face.

"Oh, I'd love to! What do you want me to do?"

"I'm taking another basket of food to Libby prison, but sometimes the guards won't let me leave the food with the prisoners. Sometimes they take it for themselves. So I'm taking along a basket of books from our library as well. The guards never want the books, only the food. But the men who are in prison with nothing to do all day are always very grateful for something to read. I'll need you to carry the second basket for me."

"Of course!" Annie was thrilled at the thought of being able to do something for the Union soldiers in the prison. She remembered what she'd heard about the Confederates breaking open the boxes sent to the Union prisoners and stealing the contents.

"Can all the soldiers read, Auntie?" She remembered how surprised she was to find out that Mary could read and write, and she'd heard talk of soldier boys right from the farms who didn't know how to do either.

"Most of the men in Libby prison can. The men in this prison are officers, and they come from families that value education. Our books have always been almost as welcome as our food, and the Confederate guards have never confiscated them."

Auntie picked up the baskets and started toward the street. "Come along, now. Take this basket and we'll be on our way. Be sure to stay close to me. The people in town are very angry at the thought of losing this war, and can't be trusted to behave as civilized human beings. We won't be in any real danger on such a short trip, but I don't want you to take foolish chances."

Annie clutched the basket of books tightly as she followed Aunt Elizabeth down the 24th Street hill to the river and then turned to her right, toward the prison. She bounced a little as she walked. This was certainly more exciting than going with Dorcas and Eliza to do household errands!

—Chapter 16

"Crazy Bett! Crazy Bett!
Bet the Yankees get you yet!"

The chanting of the town boys rang in Annie's ears as she followed Aunt Elizabeth through the crowds milling around on Cary Street as they headed toward the prison. She didn't like the chant at all, but she couldn't really blame the boys for their silly verse. She had to admit that to someone who didn't know her, Aunt Elizabeth must look very peculiar. She acted like a different person from the Auntie that Annie knew and loved. She traveled along with funny little sideways steps, her head in the ugly brown bonnet tipped to one side like a hungry robin listening for worms. As she walked behind Auntie, Annie could hear her singing a quiet little off-key tune. The words made no sense, as far as she could tell, and Auntie's voice was high and squeaky — not at all like her usual lovely low voice.

As they approached the prison, Annie suddenly realized that Aunt Elizabeth's behavior had a good reason behind it. They had moved through the crowds quickly and easily, and arrived at the prison without being jostled or delayed, and no one had reached out to try to steal the basket of food. No one wanted to get too close to Crazy Bett, just in case she wasn't as harmless as she seemed! Annie had to suppress a fit of giggles as she thought of how clever Auntie was, and how completely she was fooling all these people. As she followed quietly along, Annie kept her own head bent down to try to hide the big grin she could feel getting wider every step of the way.

At the prison the guard greeted Aunt Elizabeth like an old friend. Annie could see he thought she was a silly, harmless old lady. He was accustomed to her comings and goings and seemed glad of a break in his usual dull day.

"Hello, there, Bett! Anything tasty in that basket today?"

"Cornbread, gingerbread, cold sausages and dried apples," said Aunt Elizabeth in her strange new sing-songy voice. "Nothing fit for a man on active duty. You need good hot meals!"

"Don't I wish!" exclaimed the guard. "It'll be a cold day in July before I taste good hot food again. All I'll get for dinner is salt horse!"

Annie gasped in horror. The idea of eating horses! She thought of Chieftain and was very glad that the soldiers hadn't taken him.

"Hey, there, Missy! Don't look so worried," said the guard with a laugh. "Salt horse ain't real horse, ya know! Real horse is too valuable to eat! It's a way of trying to preserve beef so it don't go bad before ya eat it. I don't think it works, though. It's <u>bad</u>!"

He turned back to Aunt Elizabeth. "Go on in, Bett, give the poor dumb Yanks your goodies. I ain't too hungry today, anyway."

As they started toward the prison door, he reached out and took Annie by the arm.

"Not you, Missy! Ain't nobody said I should let you in! Bett, now, she's got permission. You give her your basket, and you wait here with me."

Annie looked at Aunt Elizabeth, not sure just what to do. She wasn't at all certain she wanted to stay alone with the guard, but Aunt Elizabeth nodded to her, took her basket of books, and disappeared inside the door of the big warehouse that had been turned into a prison. Annie walked a little bit away from the guard and sat down on an upturned crate to wait. She felt a little bit scared and shaky. She'd never been alone with a Confederate soldier before, and didn't know what to expect.

But the guard seemed to have lost interest in her. He'd gone over to a small group of men in the street and was standing there talking to them. She noticed that he was facing so that he could see the prison, and he kept glancing from one window to another, the whole length of the building. She wondered what he was looking for.

She tried to imagine what was going on inside the prison. She could almost see Aunt Elizabeth standing with her baskets, handing out food and books to the Yankee prisoners. She wondered how Auntie decided who received what. There certainly wasn't enough food for everyone, and only a dozen or so books.

"Oh, my!" she said out loud at a sudden thought, then looked quickly at the guard to see if he'd heard her. He was still talking to the men, paying no attention to her. She sat quietly on the crate, but her thoughts were racing.

She wondered if the book she'd read that had the message in it had been to the prison. If it had, maybe somebody there had punched the holes in those letters. Somebody who knew about General Early's march to Washington, and wanted to tell someone else about it. But who was he telling? The message certainly wasn't meant for her to find so many months later! Could it have been for Auntie?

She wriggled a little on her wooden seat, trying to get a little more comfortable. She noticed that the men had left, and the guard was leaning against a lamp post, still watching the windows of the prison. I'm glad he isn't looking at me, she thought. I wish Auntie would hurry and come out. I can hardly wait to ask her about the book.

—Chapter 17

"Auntie," Annie said as they started for home. "May I ask you something?"

Auntie's voice was soft, but firm. "Not now, Annie. This is not the time or place for discussion."

"But Auntie ..."

"I said 'No', Annie. I'll talk to you later." Aunt Elizabeth skittered along in her Crazy Bett style, and paid no more attention to Annie.

When they reached home, Dorcas met them just inside the basement door, and she and Auntie went upstairs to Auntie's bedroom. Annie followed along behind, eager to talk. But they shut the door behind them and left Annie standing in the hallway.

She stamped her foot crossly. "Now what?" she muttered. "How am I ever going to ask Auntie about the books if she won't even talk to me! Oh well," she sighed. "I might as well go find Eliza as stand here staring at a closed door. At least she'll talk to me!"

Eliza was in the carriage house, playing with the kittens and a ball, but she left them and tagged along with Annie to sit on the front steps.

The little girl was full of chatter about her trip to town with Dorcas, but Annie found it hard to be very interested in the details of the trip. Her thoughts kept turning to her own visit to the prison, and she wondered if there might be other books in the library with other messages.

Aloud, she said, "I wonder who sent the message, and why, and who did he send it to?"

"What are you talking about, Annie?" Eliza sounded puzzled. "Who sent a message, and what does it have to do with the new dress Miss Lily is going to make me for Easter? I told you I've outgrown almost all my old ones," she added proudly. "I'm almost as tall as you are now, and your old ones don't fit me anymore. That's why we had to go to the dressmaker's today." She clambered up from the bottom step to sit next to Annie. "It's going to be a blue one. I love blue."

"Blue looks nice on you," Annie said. She didn't mind that she wasn't getting a new dress too. But she did wish she'd grow more so she'd be tall someday. She'd like to be at least as tall as Auntie, even though Auntie was a small woman.

"What about the message, Annie? Tell me what message you're talking about."

"Oh, just a message I found in a book in our library. It was about the war, and I suppose some prisoner put it there when the book was at the prison a long time ago. It doesn't mean anything now, I guess." She didn't want to say too much about it to Eliza, knowing she'd have lots of questions. She herself didn't have very many answers.

"Miss Lily sends messages, too," Eliza said.

Annie stared at her in astonishment. "What do you mean? What messages? Who does she send them to?"

"I don't know who they go to," Eliza said. "But I heard her and Dorcas talking when they thought I couldn't hear them. I was looking at all the pretty ribbons, and they didn't know I was listening. I learn lots of things by listening when nobody thinks I am."

Annie looked at her in admiration. Eliza must be a lot smarter and sharper than anyone realized. Maybe she could help Annie figure out some of the things that were so puzzling. Annie began to wonder if Eliza knew anything about the strange happenings around the house. Had she heard the noises in the night, too?

"What did Dorcas and Miss Lily say?" she asked.

"I don't remember exactly, but Dorcas gave her a paper and Miss Lily said she'd put the message in a new paper pattern she was going to deliver today."

Annie thought hard for a minute. "Where do you suppose Dorcas got the message?" she asked.

"I'm not sure," Eliza said. "She and Auntie were talking before we went to town, but I was too far away to hear what they were saying."

"Auntie was probably just telling her what to do in town — what color dress to order for you, and things like that." Annie wasn't sure she wanted to confide in Eliza just yet. She thought that probably Aunt Elizabeth was part of all this message sending. But she didn't want to get Eliza involved, in case it was all Annie's own imagination. She had to talk to Auntie first. But she was certainly going to pay a lot more attention to what Eliza said from now on!

"Let's go see if Ben and Spook are back yet," she suggested. "I want to find out how Chieftain is."

She jumped down the steps and ran toward the stable, Eliza following behind like a small boat being towed by a larger one. Annie hoped Eliza would forget about secret messages for a while, at least until Annie had time to figure out some of the answers. Meantime, it was a lovely spring afternoon, and if Ben was back, maybe he'd let her ride Spook.

—Chapter 18

Ben said "No" to Annie's request to ride Spook, but she understood. Spook was an old mule, and he'd had a long, tiring trip, pulling the wagon to the farm and back. She was glad to hear Ben's report that Chieftain was fine.

Eliza wandered off, and Annie decided not to go with her. "She's probably going to play with those kittens again," she said to herself as she went back to the house. "I'd rather watch all the boats on the river."

She sat on the edge of the big back porch, swinging her feet. In her imagination she followed the river southward, past the farm, and on to City Point, near Petersburg. City Point was where General Grant was, and she knew the Union army was trying to capture Petersburg. Aunt Elizabeth had told her that if they succeeded, Confederate supplies to Richmond would be cut off, and the city and government would fall, probably ending the war.

Annie hoped it would happen soon, though Richmond might be attacked by Grant's army, with cannon balls falling all around and killing people who weren't doing any fighting. I wish there was something ordinary people could do to make peace come quicker, she thought. I bet most people wish this war was over.

She jumped a little when she heard Aunt Elizabeth's voice, and turned to greet her. No one was on the porch or in the doorway. Neither was Auntie in the yard below. Confused, Annie looked around again, then realized that the voice was coming from above. She looked up and saw that Auntie's bedroom window was open. She couldn't see into the room from where she sat, but Auntie's voice was plain and clear.

"...glad we finally have chickens and eggs again. It's not only nice to add to our diet, but it certainly makes the work go more smoothly."

Annie was bewildered. What in the world was Auntie talking about? What work? And how could chickens and eggs help in any kind of work?

She could hear another voice answering Aunt Elizabeth, but she couldn't make out whose it was or what it was saying. It must be Dorcas, she decided, since she could see Eliza practicing with her skipping rope way down on the garden path below her.

"Yes," said Aunt Elizabeth. "It must be this evening. Tomorrow could be too late."

Annie knew it wasn't right to listen to other people's conversations when they didn't know she was there. But Eliza had learned a lot by doing just that very thing. If Auntie didn't want anyone to hear what she was saying, she shouldn't talk near an open window without checking to see who was outside!

"You can pick up the basket of eggs in the kitchen right away," Auntie said to the unseen Dorcas. "If you leave now, you can be back by supper time. Here's the special egg."

Apparently she moved away from the window, because her next words were muffled and Annie couldn't understand them. But she'd heard enough to know that something very strange was going on.

I wish I could follow Dorcas and see where she's going to take those eggs, she thought. But I promised I'd never do anything like that again.

Annie wasn't surprised that Auntie would be sending eggs to someone. She was always sharing the Van Lew food with people who didn't have much, like the prisoners in Libby, and the dressmaker, Miss Lily. But what was the special egg? What could be special about an egg?

"Oh my," she gasped out loud. "Maybe it's the hollow egg that came home with us from the farm!" Auntie had never answered Annie's questions about why Matt or Mary would give them an empty eggshell, but now it was beginning to make sense. Mary had given Annie a message for Auntie, who'd said she must pass it along. And there was Eliza's story about Dorcas giving Miss Lily a message that the dressmaker was going to send along somewhere hidden in a paper pattern.

She jumped to her feet in excitement, and began walking rapidly up and down the porch. Dorcas and Auntie must be involved in passing along secret messages! Annie didn't know who they were coming from or being sent to, but it did seem as if her home was one stop on the way. She tried to think how it would work.

An important, secret message would have to be hidden so the wrong people wouldn't get it by mistake, she thought. One way to hide a message would be to have it on a small piece of paper that could be rolled up and pushed into an empty eggshell through a hole in the end! Annie almost squealed out loud as she thought about this. No one would ever think one egg in a basketful being delivered to a needy person could be so special or so important!

She skipped a little in excitement. She was bursting to share her ideas with someone, but with whom? Somehow she didn't think Auntie and Dorcas were the right ones. They might be angry she'd discovered their secret, or they might say it was all Annie's imagination. She wished Eliza were older. An older sister would be just the one to talk to. But <u>she</u> was the older sister, and it seemed as if she'd have to keep all her thoughts and excitement bottled up inside herself, while she tried to figure it all out.

—Chapter 19

From the porch Annie could see Dorcas hurrying toward the kitchen house.

I'm right, she thought. It <u>was</u> Dorcas Auntie was talking to, and now she's going to the kitchen to get the eggs. I promised I wouldn't do anything like following her to town again, but I can watch and see which way she goes!

She stood close to one of the pillars so she could hide behind it if Dorcas happened to look up toward the house, and watched as Dorcas went into the kitchen. She came out carrying a small basket and started across the yard toward the front of the house and Grace Street. Annie ducked into the house and rushed through the center hallway out onto the front porch. She arrived just in time to see Dorcas walking along the brick sidewalk toward town.

I'll bet she's going to Miss Lily's, she thought, almost bouncing in her eagerness to know where Dorcas was going. I wish I could go too! I wonder what the message is! And who will Miss Lily send it to?

She fidgeted, too restless to stay still. She jumped down the front steps and ran around the side of the house, then raced up and down the garden paths to work off some of her energy.

She didn't see Eliza anywhere. She's probably in the carriage house playing with those silly kittens, she thought as she stopped near the stable to catch her breath. But I don't think I want to talk to her now anyway. I'd rather talk to Chieftain! I wish he was here! He'd never tell anyone my secrets!

The sight of Spook standing sleepily in Chieftain's stall gave her an idea. There wasn't any reason she couldn't talk to him instead. He couldn't tell secrets either! She wriggled into the stall beside him and patted him gently. She leaned against the side of the stall and began to talk softly.

"Auntie is sending secret messages to people, Spook," she said. "I don't know who or why, but I do know Dorcas is helping her, and so is Miss Lily. I'll bet Mary is in on it too, 'cause she brought the message from the Davis house. She's probably the one who put the hollow egg in our basket. But what kind of messages could they be, and where are they going?"

She patted Spook again as he shifted his weight from one side to the other and pawed the floor softly with a front foot.

"Of course you don't know the answers," she said, but sometimes I can think better out loud, and I know you won't tell anybody what I'm thinking about!" She rubbed his nose gently for a minute. "I wish I could understand what's going on!"

"All those messages! The one about Mrs. Davis thinking the war was going to end soon, and the one at Miss Lily's. Then there's the one I found in the book. Do you suppose they're all war messages, Spook?"

"You's a right smart little lady, Miss Annie," said a voice behind her.

Annie whirled around to see who was behind Spook at the door of the stall. She threw a hand over her mouth to stifle her startled scream. It was only Ben.

"Oh, Ben! You scared me so! I didn't know anyone else was here!"

"I _lives_ here, Miss Annie! I was taking a little snooze in my room, just beyond this stall. I heard somebody talking and figgered I'd better see who 'twas. I knowed 'tweren't Spook!" She could see Ben's white teeth gleaming as his gentle black face broke into a wide grin.

Annie laughed too. But she felt a little foolish. She remembered what she'd been thinking about Aunt Elizabeth and eavesdropping, just a little while ago. Now she'd done the same thing, and talked out loud without looking to see who was around to hear her.

She shuffled her feet a little, and walked out of the stall. I wonder how much Ben heard, she thought. Did he understand? And why did he call me smart? Can he be in on the business of the messages too?

She sat down on a pile of rope coiled outside Spook's stall. "Ben, do you know anything about sending messages?" she asked.

" 'Deed I do, Miss Annie. You can send a message just about anywhere these days with this here telegraph. Gets there right quick, too. Much quicker than a letter, even if you knows how to write!" He picked up a rake and started cleaning around the doorway of the stall.

"That's not exactly what I meant. How would you send a message if you didn't want anybody to know about it?"

"Somebody's gotta know, elsewise it ain't no message!"

"Well," she explained, "I mean nobody should know but the person who's supposed to get it. A secret, sort of."

She could see the beginnings of a frown spreading across Ben's usually cheerful face.

"Who you fixing to send secrets to, Miss Annie? What kinda secrets you got, anyway?"

"Oh, nothing special," she said. "I found an old message in a book, and just wondered how it got there, and who it was for."

"I don't know nothing about books, Miss Annie. And I ain't never sent no secret messages to nobody. I heard what you was saying to Spook, just now. You're imagining things real good, but imagining don't make it true. If I was you, I'd just forgit all about such things, and go on playing and studying like little girls is s'posed to!"

"But..." Annie started. She stopped as Ben leaned the rake against the wall and walked away from her toward his room at the other end of the stable.

"He's acting just like Dorcas and Mary did when I asked them questions," she said softly to herself. "Nobody wants to tell me anything! I'll bet he knows what's going on, just like they do!"

——Chapter 20

Annie left the stable and wandered back to the house and upstairs to her bedroom, thinking hard. She pulled her best shoes from the wardrobe and fished out the messages she had hidden in a toe.

The paper with the columns of numbers still made no sense to her, but she thought it must be connected with the other messages. For one thing, it had been hidden in the hollow behind the lion's head, and why would it have been hidden if it weren't an important secret message?

The only thing that made sense was that someone was sending secret messages to Aunt Elizabeth, and she was sending them on somewhere else. The lion's head was a good place to hide such a paper until Auntie could pick it up and send it on. Maybe Dorcas had put it there.

She walked across the hall to the library and stood in the doorway, staring at the fireplace. The lion's head was right where it belonged, matching the one on the other side. She glanced over her shoulder at Aunt Elizabeth's room. The door was closed.

She stepped quickly to the fireplace and gave the lion's head a strong turn. The opening was empty. If anyone had left anything there since the paper she'd copied, it was gone now.

She closed the hiding place thoughtfully, and went over to the corner of the room where she'd found the book with the punched holes in it. She picked up another book from the same shelf and flipped through it slowly, looking for more holes. There were none, nor were there any in three other books that she checked. If any of these books had gone to the prison, they'd never been read by a person with news to send to Aunt Elizabeth.

She wondered about how many people knew about Auntie's messages. Dorcas and Mary and Miss Lily, of course. Probably Ben. And maybe Matt at the farm. Mary might have told him if he'd found out about the hollow eggs. And of course the person or people who received the messages, and anybody else who had to handle them on the way. Quite a lot of people, actually, to know a secret! It seemed as she herself must be the only one who didn't know. "I'll bet even that detective was suspicious about messages," she said to herself. "I hate not knowing what's going on!"

"Looking for something to read, Annie?"

She jumped at the sound of Aunt Elizabeth's voice, and turned around quickly. She hadn't heard Auntie's door open.

"Oh! No — I mean, yes. I mean, I don't know whether I want to read or not, but thought I had time to look before supper."

Suddenly she decided that this was the time to ask about the books that went to the prison. She reached around and pulled the Washington book from the shelf.

"Look what I found, Auntie," she said. "This book has holes punched through some of the letters, and they spell out a sentence. It's about General Early's march on Washington last summer. I've been wondering who did it and why. Was this book one you took to the prisoners once? Do you think one of them could have done it? Do you think there are others here with messages in them?"

Aunt Elizabeth took the book from her and looked at the pages Annie pointed out.

"Yes, Annie," she said. "I do remember taking this book to the prison last year. I think you're right. A prisoner probably did this."

"But who was supposed to find the holes, Auntie? Why did he do it. Surely it was meant for somebody besides me to find!"

"I'm sure of that, too," Aunt Elizabeth said with a laugh. "Prisoners don't send messages for little girls to find almost a year later! Why do you think he did it?"

Annie hesitated a minute, then decided to tell Auntie what she was really thinking. "I think maybe he was sending a message to you, Auntie. It's our book. Maybe you were supposed to find it and tell someone else!"

Aunt Elizabeth laughed again, a musical sort of chuckle that made Annie smile. "If that were true, this is quite late for me to be finding it! Much too late for me to do anything about General Early, even if I could. And you're the one who found it and showed me!"

"But who else would find a message in our book?"

"Lots of people, Annie. The books stay in the prison for several weeks, and get passed around from man to man. Our mysterious hole-puncher could have been trying to communicate with another prisoner — maybe one who was going to be exchanged and could pass the word along outside."

"But that's silly," Annie said. "All he'd have to do would be to walk up to the man when he was alone sometime, and tell him about it!"

"Maybe. But we don't know what really goes on in the prison. Maybe there are men in there that the others don't trust, and he didn't want to be seen talking to somebody they were suspicious of." Aunt Elizabeth replaced the book on the shelf and put her arm around Annie's shoulders. "Come on, let's go see if supper is ready."

"I'm glad I'm not in prison," Annie said. "I'd certainly hate to be shut up inside all the time, with nothing to do except read, even if there were lots of books."

"It's not pleasant," Aunt Elizabeth said as they walked down the stairs together. "Now they aren't even allowed near the windows. If anyone is seen looking out, the guards have orders to shoot him."

Annie remembered the guard she'd been with, who was always looking at the prison windows. She shuddered, wondering if he would really have killed a man, just for looking out a window. That would be far worse than killing someone fighting in a battle. She didn't understand how anybody could do a thing like that, even in a war.

"I wish this war would end," she said. "I wish there was something we could do to stop it! Killing somebody like that is murder, when he can't fight back!"

"War is killing people, Annie," Aunt Elizabeth said. "Thousands of brave men on both sides have lost their lives. But you have to stand up for what you believe in, even if that sometimes means fighting and killing. It's sad when people in the same country believe in different things and fight each other."

They sat down at the dining room table where Eliza was already eating her soup, and Auntie went on.

"We each have to do what we can, in our own way, to stand up for what we think is right. And I do think the war will end soon. Then we'll all have to do what we can to heal our country's wounds."

"I'm sorry I didn't wait for you," Eliza said. "I was very hungry, so Dorcas said to start."

Annie glanced sideways at Aunt Elizabeth at the end of the table. She wondered if Auntie was glad to hear Dorcas was back, with another message on its way somewhere. But Auntie's face was calm, and she appeared to be interested only in her soup.

—Chapter 21

Annie stood at the library window and stared out across the rear yard and gardens toward the river. Everything outside was gray and dreary, and a steady, cold rain poured down. It had started last night after supper, and showed no signs of stopping. Spring appeared to have left Richmond, and the heavens themselves seemed to reflect the gloom that had settled over the city. I'm glad I don't have to go outside, she thought.

She had been surprised at breakfast when Aunt Elizabeth had asked Dorcas to go into town again, this time to see what news she could hear. Auntie was a kind person, who would never send a servant out in such terrible weather unless she felt it was necessary. Especially since Dorcas had made two trips to town yesterday, to the dressmaker's and to deliver the eggs.

She heard Dorcas' voice in the hallway below, and sped headlong down the stairs. If there was important news, Annie wanted to hear it!

"Oh, Dorcas, it must have been awful walking around in this rain," she said. The maid's hair hung in damp ringlets over her forehead. "I'll bet you're glad to be back inside! What's the news? Is the war over?"

"Not yet, Miss Annie, but it won't be long, I think." Dorcas turned toward the parlor as Aunt Elizabeth came out into the hallway. "Oh, there you are, Miss Lizzie! I didn't think you heard me call you."

"Yes, I heard you, but I had something to finish first," Aunt Elizabeth said. "What did you find out, Dorcas?"

Dorcas spoke rapidly. "Mrs. Davis and the children left Richmond by train last night, they say. The whole city seems to have lost all hope of winning the war, and people think it's just a matter of days before Richmond falls, and the Confederacy with it. Jeff Davis himself has sent all the food in his house to the hospitals, and they say he's packing up all the papers in his office, ready to leave too!" She drew a deep breath. "It's spooky in town, Miss Lizzie! It's like everyone is waiting for something, but nobody knows what or when. It's a funny kind of quiet excitement that's just ready to explode, only this rain has kept it quiet today."

"What about Mary?" Annie asked, tugging at Dorcas' arm in her eagerness to know. "I'm worried about Mary! Did she go with Mrs. Davis?"

"I don't know, Miss Annie. I didn't ask about her."

"I'm sure she'll be all right," Auntie said. "If she didn't go with Mrs. Davis, she'll go out to the farm with Matt. She's loyal to the Union, and won't be in any trouble with the Federal army."

"They say Petersburg can't last much longer, Miss Lizzie," Dorcas said. "The bombardment these last few days has been something fierce!"

"I think it'll be a little while yet before the Union army takes Petersburg and comes to Richmond," Aunt Elizabeth said. "Several days, probably. But I don't think it's too soon to prepare. Dorcas, will you go to the third floor, please, and get the package from the bottom of the big, black trunk in the storeroom. Bring it down here to the parlor."

Annie bubbled with excitement as she watched Dorcas disappearing up the wide staircase.

"What's in the package, Auntie? What are we going to do to prepare? Will the army come here? Will we be bombarded too? How will the army know we're Union?"

"Questions, questions!" Auntie said with a smile. "You'll see in a minute." She stepped to the foot of the stairs.

"Eliza!" she called. "Come down here please. I want you to see this too!"

"See what, Auntie? See what?" Eliza asked as she came running downstairs. "What am I to see? I was just arranging my doll house furniture," she added. "Will this take long?"

"Not too long," Aunt Elizabeth said. "Dorcas will be back in a minute."

Annie followed Aunt Elizabeth into the parlor, staring at the large package Dorcas carried. It was square and quite thick, wrapped in newspapers, and tied with string. It looked soft, not like something in a box.

"What is it, Auntie? What is it? Open it quickly!"

"Thank you, Dorcas." Aunt Elizabeth took the package, laid it on the big round table, and untied the string. Her hands were shaking a little.

This must be really important, Annie thought.

"Here, Dorcas. Help me unfold this," Auntie said.

Annie gasped as they took the paper off a brightly colored piece of cloth.

"It's a flag!" she shouted. "An American flag! Where did we get it, Auntie? Oh, isn't it beautiful!"

"I never saw one like it," said Eliza. Auntie and Dorcas spread the huge flag out, draping it across the parlor furniture.

"There were lots of flags like this in Richmond when I was little," Annie said proudly. "I remember seeing them on the buildings when I went walking with Papa and Mama. You were too little to notice."

"Well, you don't have to brag about it," snapped Eliza. "I can't help it if I'm younger! Anyway, I can see this one now, just as well as you can!"

Annie turned to Aunt Elizabeth, who was examining the flag very carefully. "What are we going to do with it, Auntie?" she asked. "The Confederates won't want us to put it where anybody can see it!"

"No, but the Confederates won't be here much longer," Auntie said. "Dorcas, when the rain stops, I want you to get Ben and go up to the roof. The two of you can check the flagstaff and see that it's securely fastened to the chimney, and replace the ropes if they seem rotten. When the Union army comes to Richmond, I want this to be the first American flag they see!"

"Where did we get it, Auntie?" Annie asked. "Have you had it since before the war?"

"No," Aunt Elizabeth answered. "We used to fly a small one on holidays, but this is much bigger — at least twenty feet long, I should judge. I sent word to certain people that I wanted a big flag to fly when the war ended, and this was smuggled through the lines to me several months ago." She walked around the edges of the huge flag slowly.

"It seems to be all right," she said. "I don't see any sign of moth or rot."

"It's all wrinkled," said Eliza.

"That can easily be fixed," Aunt Elizabeth explained. "We'll spread it out on the dining room table and iron it. It's too big for the board in the laundry, so we'll have to bring the hot irons up here. Maybe Ben can rig up some way we can heat them here in the fireplace without getting them sooty. That would save a lot of running up and down stairs. For now, let's fold it back up and put it away. Tomorrow or Saturday will be time enough to iron it. The Federal army won't be here for a few days yet."

Annie watched Aunt Elizabeth and Dorcas fold the big flag and thought about what Auntie had said. They had this beautiful flag because she'd sent a message to someone who'd arranged to smuggle it to her. Another message! And this one involved smuggling, too!

——Chapter 22

Annie lay in bed, listening to the raindrops pattering against the windowpanes. She wasn't the least bit sleepy, in spite of the lateness of the hour. Her mind raced busily. Maybe this war was <u>really</u> going to be over soon, and her Papa would come home again. It had been so long since she'd seen him, or heard from him! Sometimes she even found it hard to remember what he looked like! Wouldn't it be wonderful to get one of his big bear-hugs again!

She was too excited to stay in bed. She slid to the floor and pulled on her robe as she left the warmth of her covers. She groped for her slippers, but couldn't find them in the dark, so she walked without them. Her toes were cold, though. She shivered a little, but she wasn't sure whether it was from the chilly air, or from her excitement at the thought of Papa coming home.

She paddled around the foot of her bed, then stopped short in surprise as she faced the door. From under the door she could see a flickering yellow light in the hallway. It cast strange moving shadows as it seemed to come and go.

Her first thought was fire! If a candle or lamp had tipped over, perhaps in the library, the draperies or papers on the desk could be burning! No one else was awake, so it was up to her to find out, wake up Auntie and Eliza, and sound the alarm!

She jerked her door open and rushed into the hallway. She turned toward the library, then stopped with a gasp. The library was completely dark, and there was no fire. But at the end of the hallway, just starting up the stairs to the third floor, she saw Aunt Elizabeth, carrying a candle in one hand, and what looked like a plate in the other!

What in the world is Auntie doing, she thought. That looks like a plate of food she's carrying. But why? Surely she can't be planning to eat it herself! She's already had a good meal with Eliza and me. Why would she be going to eat again in the attic?

As the light from the candle moved out of Annie's sight, curiosity overcame her caution. She forgot her cold bare feet as she tiptoed across the hall to the foot of the stairs and stared upwards. She could still see the flickering shadows of the candle as Auntie moved away from the top of the stairs.

For a minute Annie hesitated, remembering the strange noises she'd heard up there before. Did she dare follow up the stairs and see what was going on? Her knees shook, but she felt she <u>had</u> to know what Auntie was doing.

Silently she started up the stairs, then stopped suddenly. There were those noises again! First a scraping sort of sound, then a quiet thump. She was cold, and a little scared, but gathered her courage and continued creeping toward the top. After all, Auntie didn't seem to be afraid!

She reached the top, stepped silently into the long narrow passageway, and turned toward the wavering glow of the candle. There was Auntie, on her knees, near the old chest of drawers that held outgrown clothes. The candlestick stood on top of the dresser, but the dresser had been pulled away from the wall. Behind it was a large, black hole — almost as wide and tall as the chest itself. A similar-sized piece of wood was leaning against the wall nearby. She choked back a gasp of surprise.

She could hear Aunt Elizabeth say something very softly, but she couldn't understand the words. Then, to her shock and surprise, a face appeared in the black hole! A man's face, with shaggy hair and beard, and dark, deep-set eyes that seemed to burn in the flickering candlelight. A scrawny hand and arm reached out and took the plate Auntie was offering. Then, to Annie's horror, he looked down the hallway straight at her!

Quickly, before he could speak, she put her finger to her lips, shook her head, and fled silently back down the stairs and into her room, scrambling into bed without even taking time to remove her robe. She hoped the man wouldn't tell Auntie about seeing a little girl in nightclothes at the top of the stairs! Annie would find it hard to explain why she was wandering around in the middle of the night, even though she was pretty sure Auntie would understand her curiosity.

Her breathing gradually slowed and her shaking stopped. She lay tense and waiting, scarcely daring to move for fear Auntie would hear her and come to check on her.

──Chapter 23

In the dark quiet of her room Annie heard the scraping sound again. She heard soft footsteps on the stairs. She saw the wavering light of the candle move through the hallway. Then the light disappeared and she heard the door to Aunt Elizabeth's room close softly.

She didn't realize she'd been holding her breath till she let it out with a big sigh. She sat up in bed, pulled her knees up, and clasped her arms around them, rocking back and forth a little.

At last she knew what the strange noises were that had so frightened her earlier. Moving the dresser away from the hole made one sort of sound as it scraped across the floor. The other thumping noise must have happened when Auntie lifted the wooden cover away from the hole and set it against the wall.

But who was the man? When had he come? Why was he there? Why was he hidden in a secret room, being fed in the middle of the night? He must be a Union soldier, she thought. I wonder if he knows my Papa! Maybe he knows where Papa is, and if he's safe. I'll go ask him!

Before she could change her mind, she slid from the bed and crept quietly out into the hallway. She listened carefully for any sound from Auntie's room. Nothing. And there was no light coming from under her door. She must be safely in bed. Tiptoeing across the hall, Annie stopped by the closed door and listened again.

She breathed a sigh of relief to herself in the dark as she heard a gentle snore. Auntie was indeed in bed and asleep! Moving quickly, like a silent shadow, Annie climbed the stairs and proceeded down the hall to the chest of drawers. It was a small one, and she found she could move it quite easily. It scraped a little, and she stood very still after she'd moved it, hoping the noise hadn't waked Auntie. There were no sounds anywhere.

She looked at the wall where the chest had been, but could see no signs of where the door was. It was just too dark. How could she get it open when she couldn't even find it! Maybe the man could help.

"Hello," she called softly. "Can you hear me? Please answer!"

She could hear him moving behind the wall, then his voice came from close to the hidden door. "Who is it? What do you want?" He sounded nervous and afraid.

"I'm Annie, and I want to talk to you, but I don't know how to open the door."

Again came the cautious voice. "Who's Annie? Why do you want to talk to me?"

She hoped her voice didn't show her own nervousness. "I'm the little girl you saw at the top of the stairs earlier. I want to know who you are. Do you know how to open the door?"

He was silent for a moment, and she was afraid he wasn't going to speak to her again. Then he answered. "Down near the floor, by the baseboard, on the left side. Feel around until you find a sort of round button. Push that, and a spring will release at the bottom of the door. It'll swing out a little so you can get hold of it and lift it down. It's heavy — you might need help. I'll try to get my fingers under there too and help you hold it at first. But don't drop it and wake the whole town!"

In only a few seconds Annie had located the spring release button and freed the bottom of the door. She slid her fingers under it and pulled the door a little further out, then moved her hands around so she had one on either side of the door. It was a bit of a stretch, but she managed to lower the door enough to free the pegs on top from the holes they were fitted into in the wall above. With the man inside taking most of the weight in his hands at the bottom, they were able to move it to one side and set it carefully on the floor.

He was out in the hallway with her now, but he was sitting on the floor, and she had no idea how tall he was, but even in the dim light she could see he was very thin. She sat down next to him, panting a little from her efforts.

"So you're Annie," he said. "Glad to meet you. I'm Fred Carmichael, Union Army."

"How did you get here?" she asked.

"I was captured by the Rebs last week. They were bringing a group of us to Libby, and I decided I'd rather not go there! I'd heard Miss Van Lew was the one to see, so I slipped away from them and here I am!" He laughed a little. "This room isn't much better than a prison, I guess, but at least I'm not going to be here long. Miss Van Lew says I'll be out of here tomorrow night, and for a hiding place for a few days it could be worse!"

"My papa's in the Union Army, too," she said proudly. "Do you know him? His name is John Van Lew. My mama's dead, so that's why Eliza and I are here with Auntie. Eliza's my sister. She's seven, and I'm ten."

"I have a boy eight back home in Ohio," he said. "I sure do miss him. His name is Jimmie, and I haven't seen him in two years. But I never met your pa. Do you know whose unit he's in?"

"No. I don't even know where he is. But I think the war is almost over," she said, "so maybe you and my papa will both be home soon."

"I sure hope so! And now, Miss Annie, you'd better put me back in my hidey-hole and skedaddle back to bed. It's way past your bedtime!"

"I'm not a bit sleepy," she said, then surprised herself with a big yawn. "Well, maybe I <u>could</u> go to sleep now," she added. "Good night, Mr. Carmichael. I hope you get safely home to Ohio."

"Good night, Annie. I hope you get safely to bed." He gave a little laugh. "My, what a spanking you would have got if your aunt had turned around!"

She smiled in the darkness. "Auntie doesn't spank. But you can be sure I'd have been scolded! You won't tell on me?" she added hopefully.

"No, not this time. But don't you do this again, young lady! It's not safe for little girls to go visiting soldiers in the middle of the night. Promise?"

"I promise. If you don't tell, no one but you and I will ever know I was here. And I'll never come poking around this secret room again. I wouldn't want to give the hiding place away by accident!"

Together they put the door back in place, and when he was safely inside she snapped it shut and shoved the dresser back to its usual spot. She crept silently down the stairs and stopped at the bottom for a minute to listen. All was quiet. She peeked out into the hall, saw nothing, and darted across to her room and clambered back into bed. It felt good to cuddle down, safe and sound. She hoped Mr. Carmichael had a mattress and blankets. She supposed he did. He must not have been the first soldier to hide there if he knew about it before he came. And she herself had heard the noises before.

She rubbed her feet back and forth across the sheets to warm them, yawned again, and curled up with her pillow. Her last thoughts as she drifted off to sleep were of Auntie. Now she could add hiding escaped prisoners to sending secret messages and smuggling. She could almost see the pattern to Auntie's actions. If only she weren't so sleepy ...

—Chapter 24

In spite of her late night, Annie awoke at almost her usual time. This Saturday, April 1, was pleasant and sunny, a delightful change from the cold downpours of the previous days. She thought of Mr. Carmichael, hidden above in the secret room. She wondered if he could tell that it was a lovely day, and wished he could be outside enjoying it. It must be dreadful to have to stay hidden away in the dark! She hurried to dress and eat breakfast. She could hardly wait to get outdoors again!

Trailed by Eliza, she ran to the bottom of the garden and leaned on the wall, looking out over Main Street, towards Rocketts and the river. Everything sparkled in the morning sun like newly washed crystal. As always, people scurried about in the street below them, and boats puffed busily along the waterfront. Some of the boats put in to the docks in Rocketts, where army wagons, drays, and cannons on wheels rumbled back and forth. Annie supposed they all knew where they were going, but it just looked like a lot of confusion to her.

"It looks just the same, doesn't it?" she said to Eliza. Her little sister was eating a piece of cornbread she'd grabbed from the table as she hurried after Annie.

"Of course. Why would it be any different today?" Eliza's mouthful of cornbread made her words hard to understand.

"Don't talk with your mouth full," Annie said, trying to sound like a grown-up. "I just thought it might look different if the war is really going to end soon. Busier, perhaps. Or maybe almost nothing going on, waiting for Grant's army to come. Though I guess all the Confederates would be getting ready to fight or leave if they thought Grant was coming."

"Maybe they don't know the war is going to end." Eliza choked a little on the last of her cornbread, and Annie gave her a slap on the back. "Ouch!" Eliza howled. "You didn't need to do that!"

"If you weren't gobbling you wouldn't have choked. Of course they know the war is going to end. At least some people do. Otherwise why would Mrs. Davis have left with the children on the train the other night in all that rain!"

"Where did they go?" asked Eliza.

"I don't know. The train goes to Danville, so I guess they went there. Or maybe they want to go back to Alabama or Mississippi, wherever it is they came from."

"Will Papa be home soon?"

Annie heard the longing in Eliza's voice. "I hope so. I miss him." She turned and leaned back against the wall, staring up at the house. Meeting Mr. Carmichael last night had made her think a lot about her papa. She wondered if he had a beard like Mr. Carmichael, and if he missed his girls the way Mr. Carmichael missed Jimmie.

It would be wonderful when the war was over and all the men came back to their families again. Well, not all of them, she added sadly to herself. Some men are never going home again. I wonder if Papa is still alive and well, she thought. I hope he's not in some awful place like Libby or Andersonville in Georgia! I've heard that's worse than Libby! I wonder if Auntie knows where he is.

"You'd think with all the messages and smuggling she could have managed to arrange a letter from Papa," she muttered half aloud.

"What?" asked Eliza.

"Nothing. I was just thinking about Papa and wishing we had a letter from him." Looking at the house, she stared at the corner where the porch roof and the attic walls and roof all came together. Somewhere back in there was Mr. Carmichael. It certainly didn't show from the outside that there was a secret room there! She wondered why it had been built, and how many people had hidden there.

"Annie! Look! Here comes Mary!" squealed Eliza. She began jumping with excitement.

Annie wheeled around and looked intently at the crowds surging back and forth on Main Street. Sure enough, there was Mary's tall figure striding along from the direction of the farm, weaving in and out of the throng, and headed straight for 24th Street. As she reached the corner and started up the hill, Annie turned and ran toward the stable. "Come on!" she shouted. "Let's go meet her!"

Annie raced up the hill, Eliza not far behind, and charged through the stable yard and out onto the street.

"Mary! Mary!" She was almost dancing with joy. "I'm so glad to see you! I was so worried!" As Mary came up to her, Annie threw her arms around her and hugged as hard as she could.

"Me too! Me too!" Eliza pushed and squeezed in, till she, too, could hug Mary.

Annie heard Mary laugh happily. "What a welcome! You girls make me mighty glad I came!" She held each of them by the hand and started through the yard toward the house.

"Where've you been, Mary?" Annie asked. She skipped along. "We wondered if you went on the train with Mrs. Davis."

"No chance of that," Mary said. "She didn't want me and I didn't want to go."

"Not want you!" Eliza sounded shocked. "Why didn't she want you? You've been with her a long time."

"I was there as help in the house, to wait on tables and things like that," Mary explained. "I wasn't nursemaid for the children. So when she left the house behind, she didn't need me anymore."

"What did you do?" Annie asked. "They left a couple of days ago. Where did you go?"

"I went to the farm to see my Pa, of course. The farm is awful close to some of the Union troops these days, and I wanted to be sure he was all right. He is, so this morning I decided to come back to Richmond and see if I could be of some use to Miss Lizzie. Maybe she needs me to keep track of you two monkeys!" She laughed again, and gave each of them a swat on the bottom as they went into the house.

"Auntie!" Annie called. "Where are you? Mary's here!"

"In the library," Auntie called back. "Come on up!"

As they climbed the stairs, Annie turned to Mary with a very important question. "Did you see Chieftain? Is he safe? Is he all right?"

"He's fine. Pa takes almost better care of that horse than he does of himself!"

Annie sighed with relief. She trusted Matt to be good to Chieftain, but it was nice to hear it from someone who'd just seen him.

——Chapter 25

Annie and Eliza left Mary talking with Auntie in the library. Eliza went into her room, and in a little while, from her own room, Annie saw her running down the stairs with her skipping rope. Satisfied that everyone was busy and not paying any attention to her, she dug around in the bottom of her wardrobe, found her Sunday shoes, and pulled out the message papers hidden in the toes.

Her thoughts wandered back to the secret room and Mr. Carmichael. Auntie must have been helping Union soldiers to escape for a long time. Maybe even fugitive slaves, back before the war, right up until President Lincoln had set them free. She'd never mention the room, not even to Auntie. She wouldn't want to do or say anything that would perhaps reveal the secret and make the room useless as a hiding place.

But secret messages were a different matter, and the one from the lion's head in the library was what she herself really wondered about. She opened it up and spread it out on the bed. She studied the series of numbers carefully, for maybe the tenth time, feeling a frown wrinkling her forehead.

51111	15341	41115	35124	53515
15411	24116	16511	61246	11165
36616	34536	51514	15361	54436
30000				

What could they mean? She'd tried adding them up in all directions, but that hadn't helped. She'd tried to think of different things they could be counting, like the number of Confederate soldiers in Richmond, but even if that was what they stood for, what was it saying about them, and to whom?

She leaned on the side of her bed, paper in front of her, and thought hard. Maybe these weren't really numbers at all! Well, of course they <u>were</u> really numbers — a 5 was a 5 no matter where you found it written. But maybe they didn't <u>stand</u> for numbers. And if they didn't stand for numbers, what could they be? What else was there that people wrote. Letters, of course! And words!

When she'd first found the paper, she'd been disappointed because she'd expected to find something she could read — in words. Maybe this was a message in words after all. A message written in numbers that stood for words! Like a foreign language!

She folded up the paper and tucked it in her pocket. She ran downstairs and out onto the big back veranda, and began to walk rapidly up and down.

She felt a little foolish that she hadn't thought of a different language a long time ago. She herself had begun to study French just last year. And music was like another language too. Now if she could just translate these numbers!

She sat down on the edge of the porch and began to swing her legs slowly back and forth. She took another look at the paper. If this was a kind of alphabet, it was a strange one. There were no 7's or 8's or 9's, and all the zeros were at the end. She'd never heard of an alphabet with just six letters. But then, she sighed to herself, I suppose the world is full of things I've never heard of!

She put the paper back in her pocket. She'd figure out a way to read it somehow, but she might need help. She wandered back into the house and stood at the bottom of the stairs. Shall I ask Auntie? she said to herself. She must be able to read this, or why would anyone send it here? It's a good way to pass along a secret message. Even if the wrong people managed to get hold of it, they couldn't read it any better than I can.

Everyone in Richmond who knew Elizabeth Van Lew knew how she felt about the war. She was for the Union, and against slavery, and her brother, Annie's papa, was fighting on the Federal side. She took books and food to the prisoners in Libby, and lots of people thought she was crazy.

Annie smiled in secret delight as she thought about the Confederate people in Richmond and what they didn't know about Auntie. Nobody knew about the secret room and the hidden soldiers. Nobody knew about the secret messages and the smuggled flag. Auntie was a true United States patriot, doing what she could to help her country, just like the heroes of the Revolution — George Washington, and Thomas Jefferson, and Paul Revere. Even like Nathan Hale of Connecticut, who'd given up his life for his country when the British caught him spying.

Annie gave a sudden gasp, and sat down hard on the bottom step. Auntie might be a spy for the Union, but were the Confederates sure of it? They must suspect, or why else did they send a detective to follow her. Could they prove it? What would happen if they found out for sure Auntie was a spy? Would they hang her, like the British had hung Nathan Hale? What would happen to Annie and Eliza if they did? Would the war end soon enough so that Auntie wouldn't be caught? What would happen to Mary, and Dorcas, and Miss Lily? Would they kill them too? And what about Matt and Ben?

—Chapter 26

Sunday, April 2, was another beautiful spring day, the loveliest of the year so far, but Annie was too nervous and tense to enjoy it. She was very worried. She'd lost her appetite and didn't want any breakfast. She left the table without finishing. She wasn't hungry, even though she hadn't eaten her supper the night before. The hard knot in her stomach was too big. I didn't sleep very well last night, either, she thought. I hope Auntie thinks I'm coming down with something. I'm not at all sure I want her to know what's really bothering me.

She worried about whether the Confederates would think she and Eliza were spies too. "And I sort of am," she said softly to herself as she walked slowly down the garden path, scuffing her feet. "I know some of the secrets, and I helped pass on a message. And Eliza knows about Dorcas and Miss Lily. What if they caught us! Would they kill little girls?" That was an awful scary thought!

As she leaned against the wall at the bottom of the garden, she noticed how calm everything was in the street below. Not like the usual weekday hubbub. The few people she could see were either strolling along slowly, or just standing in the spring sunshine. Birds were chirping, and bees were buzzing, and the gentle breeze was rustling the baby leaves on the trees. But something was missing.

"Of course!" she said aloud. "There isn't any gunfire today! I wonder why it's stopped. It was so heavy yesterday, from down near Petersburg, when Dorcas and Mary were ironing that beautiful flag. The noise of the guns never seemed to stop! Maybe the war is over! Maybe we're all safe now!"

But inside she still felt scared. "I wish I knew what to do," she said, turning away from the wall and starting back up through the gardens. "I'd like to talk to somebody about this. But who? Eliza'd just get scared too. Dorcas and Mary would tell me to stop imagining things. I guess I'd better talk to Auntie."

Somehow, just making the decision to confide in Auntie made her feel much better. She even began to feel hungry, and wondered how close it was to dinner time. She ran the rest of the way up to the house and hurried in through the basement door under the big back porch.

Auntie, Mary, and Dorcas were standing together talking just inside the door. "I want you two to go into town this afternoon," Aunt Elizabeth was saying. She looked up as Annie came in, and smiled at her. "Don't ask to go too, Annie. The answer is no."

She turned back to the two waiting women. "Separate, and go into different areas. Listen a lot, and ask questions of anyone you know — or anyone else who seems to know what's happening. Something is going on, and we need to know what it is. Try to find out what it means that there's no gunfire today, and why everything seems so unusually quiet. Stay as long as you think it's useful, but I'd suggest you get back before dark."

"Yes, Miss Lizzie," they said at almost the same time. "Will you be all right here alone?" added Dorcas.

"I'm not alone!" Auntie smiled at Annie again. "Annie will be here with me, and who would want to bother me anyway? No one wants to have anything to do with Crazy Bett!"

—Chapter 27

Later, as they finished dinner, Aunt Elizabeth turned to Eliza. "I want you to do something for me this afternoon, Eliza," she said. "Take your skipping rope, or some dolls, and go down to the bottom of the garden. Perhaps you could have a tea party for the dolls in the gazebo. While you're there, I want you to keep an eye on Main Street and what goes on there. If you see anything different or strange, I want you to come and tell me at once. Can you do this for me?"

"Of course, Auntie!" Eliza seemed almost ready to explode with importance. "I'll get my things right now!"

As Eliza ran out of the dining room, Aunt Elizabeth leaned back in her chair and looked at Annie. "All right, Annie. We're alone now, and we will be for quite a while, unless something unusual happens on Main Street, which I don't expect. Do you want to tell me what's bothering you? You haven't been your usual self at all the last day or two!"

"Oh, Auntie!" Annie began. She hadn't expected a good chance to talk so soon, and wasn't ready.

She didn't even know where to begin. "I'm scared! Are you a spy? Will they hang you?" The words trembled as they left her lips.

She could see by the look on Aunt Elizabeth's face that she was both surprised and concerned by what Annie'd said. But Auntie didn't look angry, and she didn't look as if she thought Annie was just imagining things, either.

"Why do you ask that, Annie?" The words came gently. "Why do you think I'm a spy?"

"So many things — messages, and the smuggled flag, and... "Annie stopped short. She'd promised never to mention the secret room.

"Tell me about it," Auntie said, her voice still calm.

"Well," Annie began. "There was the message in the library book — and there might have been other ones too, but we have so many books I couldn't find another. And you go to Libby so often — the men there could tell you lots of things. And there was the hollow egg. It would be easy to hide a message in an eggshell, and I heard you and Dorcas talking and saw her take it to town. And the detective thought he was following you when Dorcas went to Miss Lily's. And the other time when she and Eliza went for Eliza's new Easter dress and Eliza said she heard them talking then ..." She stopped again. She hadn't meant to bring Eliza into the story.

"Anything else?" Auntie asked softly.

Annie brought out her own words carefully. "The message that Mary brought about Mrs. Davis that you said had to be passed on to other Union people. And the way you act crazy in front of people when I know you're not — like you're trying to fool them so they won't suspect you. Everybody knows we're Union, so they might think you were trying to help if they didn't think you were crazy."

Once she started talking she couldn't seem to hold anything back. All the ideas and fears that had been kept inside for weeks came pouring out like water rushing through a burst dam.

Then she saw that Aunt Elizabeth was smiling at her.

"You're a very observant and thoughtful girl, Annie Van Lew," Auntie said approvingly. "You have a good, logical mind, and when you notice things you try to make sense out of what you see. That's a fine ability to have. I can certainly understand why you might think I'm a spy. I'm just glad the Confederates don't seem to think as clearly as you do! I wouldn't want to be put in prison or hanged!" She laughed a little. "Any other clues you've discovered to link me with a spy ring?"

Annie was thinking more calmly and clearly now, and Auntie's last question made her realize that there was a purpose behind what she was asking. She wanted to find out everything that Annie knew or suspected. She wanted to know what might be known or imagined by the enemy — the Confederates. If Annie herself could discover something, so could a clever adult.

If Auntie was really a spy, then for her safety she needed to have Annie be completely honest. Well, almost completely. She wouldn't break her promise to Mr. Carmichael. "There is one more thing," she said. "Come on upstairs and I'll show you."

Upstairs she went into her bedroom, while Auntie waited in the doorway. She fished her shoes from the wardrobe and pulled out the hidden paper, then led Auntie into the library.

"There's a secret hiding place in here, and I found a secret paper in it. But I can't read it — it's all numbers." Going over to the fireplace she twisted the lion's head and showed Aunt Elizabeth the hidey-hole, then handed her the wrinkled, folded paper she's studied uselessly so many times.

Auntie frowned. "How did you find this?"

"It was an accident. I was angry one day and threw a book and it hit the lion's head and turned it. I was curious, so I looked again another day, and found a paper like this. I copied the numbers, but they don't make any sense. It's like trying to read when you don't know the language!"

"This is apparently written in what is called a code," Aunt Elizabeth explained. "You're right that it's like another language, but if you have the key to the code you can read and write in it easily."

"Can you read this?" Annie asked hesitantly.

"If I had the key with the message, yes, and so could you. But people who use codes are very careful to keep the keys secret, or the code wouldn't be of any use."

"But Auntie! How could a code message get into our library if somebody in this house didn't have the key?"

Aunt Elizabeth laughed softly. "I said you had a logical mind! You've just proven it again! You're right, Annie, dear. Someone does. But I don't think you need to know just who it is. It might not be safe."

"I wish I knew what it said," Annie said wistfully.

"That can be arranged. It's an old message by now, and with the war nearly over it won't matter if you know what it says. You come open the lion's head after supper — just you alone, don't let Eliza know — and I'll see that a translation of the message is hidden there for you to find. You read it, then destroy it. We don't want to leave any evidence for the enemy!"

—Chapter 28

Annie and Aunt Elizabeth walked down the front stairs together and went out onto the sunny rear porch. To their surprise Eliza was running up the hill toward the house as fast as she could, waving her arms and shouting as she came. A doll hung upside down by one leg in her left hand, jouncing up and down with the motion of Eliza's arms as she pounded up the hill.

"Auntie! Auntie!" she yelled as she saw them. "Come see! Something's happening!"

Aunt Elizabeth hurried back into the house, down the rear stairs and out the ground floor basement entrance, with Annie right behind her.

"You told me to watch and I did, and I was to tell you if I saw something and I did, and — Oh please come see!" Eliza was panting and puffing, jumping about on the path like a lively cricket.

"Calm down, Eliza," Auntie said. "I can't understand you when you babble. Now, what do you want me to see?"

Eliza grabbed Aunt Elizabeth with her free right hand and started tugging her down the path. "Hurry! Hurry! Come see!"

"See what? What's happening?" Annie tossed the questions over her shoulder, racing past them as they hurried down the hill, but she didn't wait for answers.

When she reached the garden wall she gawked in amazement at the scene below her. Main Street, so quiet that morning, was packed with people — soldiers, women, children, blacks, old men — all moving west. Some were pulling all sorts of wagons and carts, loaded with a hodge-podge of belongings, piled every which way. Most did not even stop to pick up things that fell from the untidy heaps. Others were struggling along with their arms full of as many things as they could carry. Women were clinging to soldiers, who carried packs on their backs. There were people everywhere, all fleeing toward the west in a huge mass that made travel through the street almost impossible. The crying of small children rose above the general rumble of noise.

"Oh, my!" Annie gasped. "What's happening, Auntie?"

"I don't know for sure, girls," Aunt Elizabeth answered slowly, "but it looks as if Richmond is being evacuated. That means people are leaving the city, Eliza," she added before Eliza could get the question out. "And look over toward Rocketts! There are hundreds of prisoners being herded toward the docks! They must be going to send them down the river in an exchange program. They usually do that only in the middle of the night."

Annie wondered for a brief second how Auntie would know that, but her real question was "Why". "Why are they doing it, Auntie? Why is everybody leaving, and why are they exchanging prisoners before they go?"

"I think the Yankees will be here very soon," Auntie answered, and Annie could hear the excitement in her voice. "The soldiers are leaving in hopes they can fight again somewhere else. The civilians don't want to be here when the Yankees arrive. I imagine the prisoner exchange is because if the Yankees set them free, there won't be any Confederates released from northern prisons. The Rebs will need all the released prisoners they can get to keep fighting!"

"Will everybody leave?" Eliza's words seemed to pop out.

"No indeed," said Auntie. "The people who lived here before the war will probably stay. And so will the people who have sense enough to realize that there isn't anywhere else to go. Everyone's heading for the Danville Depot, and there'll never be enough train cars to hold them all! They won't be any better off outside Richmond anyway. At least here they have beds and some food. Those who manage to leave will be scattered all over the countryside west of here scavenging like a plague of locusts!"

"We'll stay here, won't we?" Eliza sounded doubtful.

"Of course, silly!" Annie answered her. "This is our home, and we're on the Union side. We <u>want</u> the Yankees to come! Besides," she added, "how could Papa ever find us if we left?"

Auntie spoke quickly. "Come on back to the house, girls," she said. "This scene will go on for hours, and I want to be at the house when Dorcas and Mary come back. "They'll certainly have news for us!"

As they walked slowly up the hill, Eliza beamed with pride and importance. "You asked me to watch, Auntie! Didn't I do a good job? How did you know I was needed to watch and tell you what I saw?"

"I knew something might happen sometime, and wanted to be sure I heard about it. You did a fine job. Thank you!"

Annie glanced at Auntie's face and grinned, as Auntie gave her a big wink. She knew she'd only been sending Eliza away so they could talk! She hadn't really thought anything would happen at all. Annie was happy for Eliza that something <u>had</u> happened so that she could feel involved and important.

Her own fears had almost disappeared. If the Federal troops were so close that people were leaving Richmond, there didn't seem to be much chance of the Confederates finding out that Aunt Elizabeth was a spy. They'd be too busy running! But seeing that mob as it pushed west was scary. I hope they stay away from Church Hill, she thought.

Dorcas and Mary had not yet arrived home when they reached the house. Auntie went in. Eliza remembered she'd left most of the doll tea party still in the gazebo, so she said she was going back to get them, and maybe watch the street crowds a while longer. Annie chose to sit on the porch and watch the river while she waited for the servants to return.

There seemed to be a lot of activity among all the boats. She wondered whether they were planning to leave too. But where could they go? The river was filled with rapids and falls to the west, and downstream led straight to the Yankees. Maybe Dorcas and Mary would be able to tell them what was going on.

It was nearly suppertime before the two women came, and they were bubbling over with information.

"Oh, Miss Lizzie," Dorcas began. "Richmond has just gone crazy! Mr. Davis was called out of church this morning by a message from General Lee that he couldn't hold the lines any longer, and the government should leave tonight! All the soldiers and sailors are ordered to leave too. Everyone is scrambling to get out of town with whatever they can take with them. All the government offices are being emptied, and hundreds of boxes are being carted to the depot."

Mary spoke quickly, as Dorcas paused for breath. "There are fires in the streets, burning everything that can't be carried away. They're giving away all the supplies in the Commissary, and people are grabbing anything they can lay hold of! Barrels of flour, hams, sugar, coffee, all sorts of clothes — anything! I never knew there was so much food here!

All these months people have been hungry while this food has been hidden away! It's wrong!"

Dorcas continued. "People are breaking into stores all over the place — stealing jewelry, clothes, anything they can carry! And the shopkeepers are all rushing to leave town. They don't even seem to care! The banks are all crowded with people trying to get gold and silver for their Confederate money. I don't guess that's going to be worth anything very much longer! And Oh, Miss Lizzie! The streets are just running with whiskey! The government wanted all those barrels of liquor thrown out so people wouldn't go on a drunken spree. But they're getting it right out of the gutter! With their hands, if they haven't anything else to catch it in! The government and important people are all scrambling to get out, and all the trash are stealing and getting drunk! It's a right scary place to be!"

Annie and Eliza sat together on the horsehair sofa in the parlor as they listened to the women describe the frantic scene in Richmond. Auntie was nearby in an embroidered arm chair, nodding her head every now and then at something she heard.

"Will we be in any danger here?" asked Annie, her heart thumping with excitement and fear. She remembered the milling crowds on Main Street and worried about what they might do. "Will all these wild people come up on Church Hill?"

Aunt Elizabeth laughed. "I doubt it! Even in Richmond whiskey won't flow up hill, and that's what most of them are looking for. As long as we stay in our own house we should have little trouble."

Annie looked at Auntie. I wonder what Auntie really means, she thought. Maybe she's just trying to keep me and Eliza calm. Does she really believe what she's saying? There was a sense of danger and excitement that Auntie couldn't completely hide, in spite of her attempt to be reassuring. Annie's stomach was churning and her hands and feet felt icy as she sat there, wondering if Auntie could protect them if the mob came.

—Chapter 29

I can't sit still, Annie thought, as the evening hours slowly passed. I keep waiting for something to happen, but I don't know what! She paced around the house, tried to read, toyed with the piano, but couldn't settle down to anything.

She went out onto the back porch and listened to the racket from the street below. The noise was unending — shouts, curses, some shots, the rumble of cannon being pulled along, distant whistles screeching, horses neighing, wagons and drays bumping over cobblestones. It seemed to her like something from the Bible, a confused roar such as might be heard as everyone tried to escape Judgment Day. The wavering glow of fires burning off toward the west added an eerie look that made the whole scene with its background of constant uproar seem like something from a nightmare. She went back into the quiet of the house and heaved a sigh of relief, glad to escape the constant din outside.

The parlor was empty when she returned from what she decided would be her last trip out onto the porch. Nothing was changing outside, and she didn't want to be alone. I'm safer inside, she thought. I wonder where everyone is. She turned back into the hallway, and saw Aunt Elizabeth coming down the stairs.

"Any change outside?" Auntie asked.

"No, just the same. Where's everybody?"

"Dorcas and Mary have gone to their rooms to try to get some sleep. They've had a very tiring day. Eliza fell asleep on the sofa, so I've just carried her up and tucked her in. How about you?"

"I'm not sleepy. I don't really know what I want to do. I don't want to go out anymore, but I don't want to just sit in here, either. I keep expecting something to happen."

Auntie's voice was calm, but it held an undertone of excitement. "You're living through an important moment in history, Annie. Something is indeed going to happen. Something that will be written up in all the history books in the future. I think you're witnessing the end of this terrible civil war, and the fall of the Confederate States of America. God willing, our Union has been preserved!"

Aunt Elizabeth crossed the room and sat in the big armchair. She pulled a small table close to her. "Why don't you go up to the library and get the checker board. Then you and I can sit and play checkers while history is being made! Don't bother to take a candle — there's a lamp burning on my desk. Put it out when you leave, please."

Annie scurried up the stairs and into the library. She started toward the checker board on the table, then turned and rushed over to the fireplace. She'd almost forgotten about the message hidden in the lion's head! She opened the hiding place and pulled out a small scrap of paper. She spread it out on the desk in the lamp light, and read the message.

LEE APPEALS ALL DESERTERS RETURN FULL PARDON

In spite of the excitement, Auntie had remembered to have the message translated for her. And of course Auntie was right. It was an old message that wouldn't matter now, no matter who read it. Annie was happy to know what it said, finally, even if she didn't have the key. She didn't suppose there would be any need to write coded messages anymore, now that the war was ending. But she still wondered who sent it, and where it had gone from Grace Street.

She gathered up the checkers and checker board, blew out the lamp, and hurried downstairs to join Aunt Elizabeth. It made her feel very grown-up to be staying up without one word being said about bedtime. Somehow Auntie understood what Annie was feeling this historic night, and she thought that maybe Auntie was glad of her company too, so that she didn't have to be alone either.

"What will happen when the war is over, Auntie?" she asked as they set up the game board. "What will happen to all those people trying to get away from here?"

"I don't know, Annie. I suppose eventually they'll go back to their homes and try to pick up their lives where they left off. It won't be easy. So much of the south has been destroyed — homes and farms burned, young men killed. I'm afraid there are hard times ahead."

"It's too bad that when someone wins, someone else has to lose. I'll be glad when it's all over and we can be friends again. But I'm glad we're the ones who are winning!"

Auntie laughed. "So am I! This division of our country has been a dreadful thing, and it will be wonderful to be united again. Now let's see who's going to win at checkers!"

As midnight approached, Annie felt herself beginning to droop, even though she had won six games. She smiled at Aunt Elizabeth. "I guess I'd better go to bed now. I don't think I could manage to play even one more game, much less win it!"

Auntie began to put the game away. "Run along, honey. Get what sleep you can. Morning will be here soon, and tomorrow may be a long, busy, exciting day. I'm going to try to get some rest myself."

Once in bed, Annie dropped off to sleep quickly, but she awoke often, disturbed by the noise outside her window. In spite of the lateness of her bedtime the night seemed endless and the minutes crept. Each time she woke she was surprised to find it was still dark. Would morning never come!

Suddenly, a violent explosion shook the house. Windows rattled and cracked. Annie found herself sitting on the floor beside her bed, with echoes of the blast still ringing in her ears. Someone nearby was screaming. It must be Eliza! She scrambled to her feet, and her heart pounded as she raced across the hall to Eliza's room. To her relief she saw Auntie hurrying toward her, candle in hand.

"Auntie! What happened? Eliza! Are you all right?" In the candlelight she could see Eliza on the floor. Her screams had changed to deep, gasping sobs. Annie dropped down and gave her a tight, comforting hug.

Auntie put the candle on the dresser. "Are you hurt, Eliza, or just frightened?" she asked.

Annie could feel Eliza shaking as she held her, but the little girl's sobs were softer. "I - I - I think I'm all right," she gulped. "What happened? Is our house on fire? Shouldn't we hurry and get out?"

"No, we're not on fire," Aunt Elizabeth said. "It was an explosion outside. Let's go into my room and see if we can see anything from my windows."

As they looked out toward the river they could see flames from a ship. Their long fingers reached toward the sky, and the fire lighted up the night. Great clouds of black smoke drifted slowly on the wind.

"It's the *Patrick Henry*!" Auntie exclaimed. "The rebels must have blown up their own ship! That's the school ship they use for training their navy recruits, Eliza. All the other gunboats moved on down the river earlier. They must be desperate indeed to destroy their own ship that way!" She sounded elated. "The Union troops must surely be close!"

Auntie picked up her watch from the bedside table. "Three o'clock! We'd better head back to bed, girls, and get what sleep we can before daylight. We want to be ready and waiting when our Yankee boys come!"

Back in bed Annie dozed, but she couldn't fall into a deep sleep. She was too tense, and there were still explosions in the distance. Probably the gunboats down the river were being destroyed too. At least they were far enough away so that she didn't get thrown out of bed again, even if she couldn't sleep much!

Finally she heard Auntie moving about, so she decided to get up too. As she pulled on her petticoat, she glanced out her window toward the downtown section of Richmond. Half dressed as she was, she ran into the hall. "Auntie! Eliza! Come see!" she yelled. "Richmond is on fire! It's all burning up!"

She could hear them behind her as she galloped up the stairs to the third floor, then out through the small door leading to the roof. The scene before her was like a painting of the fires of Hell. "Oh, Auntie! The whole business section is burning! How could that happen?"

She could feel Aunt Elizabeth's hand tremble on her shoulder as she stood behind her. "I think the rebels set these fires themselves," Auntie said. "See! The Iron Works are burning, and all the tobacco warehouses, and the flour mills. They didn't want to leave anything behind that the Union troops could use. But that fire is spreading fast! Look! Even the bridges are blazing!"

"Will the fire come here?" asked Eliza. Her voice sounded frightened.

"We hope not. The wind isn't blowing this way just now. But it won't be any easy job to put it out, or even to keep it contained in the downtown area. We'll have to keep a close watch on it. Meantime, let's finish dressing and get some breakfast."

Downstairs, they met Dorcas at the door of the dining room. She looked tired, and Annie guessed that she and Mary hadn't slept much either.

Auntie smiled at Dorcas. "Thank you and Cook for having our food ready so early," she said. "Now I have another task for you. The time has come to raise our flag! The Federal troops should be here soon, and we want to be sure they see our Stars and Stripes when they come!"

—Chapter 30

Annie found out that the Federal troops were not the first ones to see the Van Lews' flag flying from the rooftop! Just as she was finishing her breakfast, she heard an uproar from the street in front of the house. She ran into the hallway just in time to see Aunt Elizabeth step out onto the front porch. Even from inside, Annie could see that the crowd outside was angry. Men were yelling, shaking fists, throwing rocks. Someone in the crowd yelled, "Burn the Yankee-lover's house down!" Auntie might be hurt!

Annie grabbed Eliza by the hand and dragged her up the stairs.

"Come on! Pack our things and get them out in the garden! If the house burns we won't have time to save anything!"

She tumbled most of her clothes into a carpet bag. Then she dragged a sheet from her bed for the rest, and added some of her treasured possessions and books to the pile. As she struggled down the stairs with her bundles, Annie could see Aunt Elizabeth still on the porch. She stood straight and proud by the iron railing at the front edge of the porch as she pointed directly at certain people in the street before her.

Her voice rang out over the roar of the mob. "I know you, Dan Quigley! And you, Tom Matthews! And you, Peter Ridgeway! You too, Billy Thompson! Grant's troops will be here any minute now. If this house is harmed in any way, yours will all be burning before noon! Every house in this neighborhood will follow!"

The noise from the mob dropped to a low, muttering grumble, and the men began drifting away. Annie watched in fascination as they left. Auntie still stood firm on the porch, even her back showing her pride and determination.

Imagine breaking up an angry crowd just by talking to them, thought Annie! What a strong, wonderful person Auntie is. To think anyone would call her "Crazy Bett"! I hope I grow up to be just like her!

Aunt Elizabeth turned and came in, and gave a laugh as she saw Annie and Eliza with their bundles.

"All right girls! Back upstairs with your treasures! We won't be burned today!" She seemed excited and calm at the same time.

Annie ran to her and gave her a big hug. "Oh, Auntie! I love you so much!"

Auntie squeezed her back, hard.

"I love you too, Annie. Now get these things back where they belong. We can't have them here cluttering up the front hall if General Grant should come!"

Annie laughed at the idea of General Grant coming to their house in the middle of capturing Richmond, but she hurried to drag her lumpy bundles back upstairs, just in case.

Later, she stood on the big back porch with Eliza and watched the smoke and flames billowing over Richmond. It was an awesome, scary sight. Suddenly she heard band music coming from the direction of Rocketts. They raced to the bottom of the garden and leaned against the wall. Annie's heart was almost dancing with joy. There, marching along Main Street, came the Yankee troops, and the band was playing Annie's well-loved *Yankee Doodle*!

"Oh, I hope Papa is with them!" she said as she squeezed Eliza's hand. "But I don't suppose so. We'd have heard if he'd been as close as Petersburg. He might even have tried to sneak through the lines to see us." Even without her papa they were a thrilling sight to see, and looked strong and well-fed.

Auntie joined them, and they watched till most of the troops had passed. Then the three of them hurried down onto Main Street to mingle with the proudly marching men. Aunt Elizabeth wore a big bonnet, not her Crazy Bett bonnet but a beautiful one she'd been saving for a special occasion. The bright pink silk flowers stood out gaily against the dark green velvet, and Annie thought it was the prettiest hat she'd ever seen. Auntie laughed and chattered as she greeted the soldiers. She even hugged the horses! Annie had never seen her so happy!

She herself was thinking one mixed-up thought after another. When would Papa come home, and how long was Richmond going to burn, and would the fire come close to them, and, now that the war was ending, Chieftain could come back from the farm, and maybe she and Eliza would have friends to play with. She even felt a touch of sorrow for Maggie Davis. She must be so sad, Annie thought, now that her father's side has lost the war.

But this was not a day for sadness! She skipped happily along at Auntie's side, admiring the soldiers and their well-fed horses, and trying to imagine how different their life would be from now on. Then Auntie spoke to her.

"Go home, Annie, and hitch up Spook to the wagon if Ben isn't there to do it." Auntie's voice was tense with suppressed excitement. "Then drive back toward town, and I'll meet you somewhere along Broad Street. I still have work to do!"

As Annie drove proudly along Broad Street she was grateful she'd had experience driving before, even if driving to the farm was a lot easier than this! She was pleased Auntie trusted her to do this, but she wondered what Auntie was talking about. What work could she possibly have to do in a burning city? Work that needed a wagon!

When she found Auntie and Eliza and they climbed into the wagon with her, she wasn't sorry to turn the driving over to Auntie. She'd loved doing it! It made her feel very grown-up. But as they went through town, winding their way through streets still crowded with people of all ages and sizes, surrounded by heaps of belongings of all descriptions, with fires not far away, and the air filled with drifting smoke that burned and stung her throat, she was glad Auntie was in charge of Spook and the wagon.

It was late afternoon before they finally turned homeward. Annie knew now why they'd needed the wagon. They'd driven to almost all the government buildings in Richmond! They'd entered the Capitol, even its library, and prowled through dozens of other buildings, with Auntie feverishly searching through drawers and cupboards, loading all sorts of papers and boxes into their wagon. What had she been looking for, Annie wondered?

They went to the Executive Mansion, which was burning in several places, and watched while a faithful gardener managed to extinguish the flames before much damage was done. Then they moved on without going in. At the Governor's Mansion Eliza found a little lost dog, and pleaded with Auntie to be allowed to take him home. The frantic owner solved that problem by appearing, clutching him tight, and scurrying away with him. Eliza seemed to be too tired and overcome by the day's experiences to be very upset at losing him.

Annie realized she was ravenously hungry! They'd had no dinner, and breakfast had been very early. Her mouth watered as she thought about supper when Auntie turned toward home.

To Annie's surprise, a small group of Union soldiers rode up to them and stopped them. "Miss Van Lew?" the leader asked.

"Yes, sir," Aunt Elizabeth answered. "What do you want with me?"

"We're a guard unit, sent by General Grant to see to your safety." He laughed. "We expected to guard a house. We didn't anticipate chasing a mobile unit! We've been trying to catch up with you all day!"

"Well, now you have!" Auntie smiled up at him from under her big flowered bonnet. "You have found us, and now you may escort us home!"

As they drove back to the house on Grace Street, the wagon bumping over the cobblestones, the horses' hooves clumping beside them in a steady clop-clop, Annie looked at Aunt Elizabeth in wonder. Maybe she hadn't been joking about General Grant seeing the clutter in their hallway! How could he know anything about Auntie, and why did he think she'd need a guard? Was it possible that Auntie and General Grant knew each other?

Back at the house the soldiers led their horses into the stable yard, and one of them volunteered to help Ben take care of Spook. Annie, Eliza, and Aunt Elizabeth went into the house and gratefully ate the cold meal Dorcas and Mary set before them. Annie was tired, but still eager to know what was going to happen next. Eliza looked almost dazed, and Auntie seemed to radiate with an inner glow.

Just as they finished eating, the front door bell rang, and Annie heard someone going to open it. A minute later Dorcas appeared in the dining room doorway. "You have a guest, Miss Lizzie. I showed him into the parlor."

"Thank you, Dorcas. Come along girls, let's see who's here."

When she entered the parlor, Annie saw a tall, uniformed officer, who stood erect, hat in hand. He bowed to Aunt Elizabeth.

"Miss Van Lew? Major General Godfrey Weitzel at your service." He paused, then turned toward Annie and Eliza. "And who are these charming young ladies?"

Annie dropped her best curtsy. "I'm Annie Randolph Van Lew," she said proudly, "and this is my sister, Eliza Louise." She reached to take Eliza's hand as she presented her. But Eliza had apparently been overcome by a fit of shyness and was hiding behind Auntie's skirts!

Auntie laughed and pulled Eliza forward. "Say hello to General Weitzel, Eliza," she said. "Then you may leave."

Eliza ducked her head, muttered something no one could understand, and fled out the door. Annie could hear her thumping up the stairs as fast as she could go. But Annie wanted to know what was going on, and she had no intention of leaving if she didn't get sent away. She slipped quietly over to the sofa and sat there to listen.

"... sorry I could not visit you sooner," the general was saying. "When the mayor met me before dawn on the Petersburg road and asked me to take over the city, I knew I'd be a very busy man. We had to put down riots, extinguish fires, and take the city in control. We declared martial law. Not much time for calling on charming ladies! Did the guard troops find you?"

"Yes indeed," answered Auntie. "I'm grateful to General Grant for thinking of it, and I have a wagonload of Confederate materials and information he may find interesting."

"It will be a while before he can examine it, I imagine. He's chasing off to the west after General Lee. If they catch up before Lee can join Johnston, this war will be over! But he did send you a message. He said to tell you that of all the information he received from Richmond during the war, yours was the most valuable."

Annie didn't hear Aunt Elizabeth's answer. She was thinking that everything seemed so simple, now that she knew! Auntie was indeed a spy, and must have been for years! Her secret messages had gone to General Grant, the head of the whole Union army! Auntie gathered information everywhere she could, and sent it on to the man who was leading the fight to save the country she loved.

The Confederates must have suspected. After all, they'd sent the detective! But they never knew for sure. Most people just thought of Auntie as Crazy Bett. Now it was over, and Auntie was safe! Yet busy as she must have been with spying, she'd still had time and energy left over for loving and caring for Annie and Eliza.

The general turned to leave, and Auntie walked beside him to the door. Annie could hardly take her eyes off him. He was the first general she'd ever seen! He was tall and straight, and his uniform was neat and clean, not all muddied and rumpled like the regular soldiers she'd seen that afternoon. She wondered if even General Grant would look so impressive!

Auntie returned to the parlor and smiled at Annie. "So now you know!"

"Yes, now I know," said Annie. She thought she'd burst with love and pride. "I know you're the most wonderful Auntie in the world, and that you stood up for what you believed in, no matter what, and did everything you could to help save our country! I know I love you and want to be just like you. Except..." She hesitated a moment. "Except I still hope I grow to be taller than you!"

They both laughed, and Auntie grabbed Annie's hands, pulling her to her feet. They grinned at each other in delight as they danced around the room together, merrily singing *Yankee Doodle.*

WHAT HAPPENED AFTERWARD

Annie's papa came home safely from the war, and several years later remarried and raised a second family of five children.

Aunt Elizabeth was rewarded for her services to General Grant and the United States by being named postmistress of Richmond when he became President. But her neighbors in Richmond never forgave her, and always considered her a traitor to the cause of the Confederacy.

Eliza never married, but continued living with Auntie until they both died in the year 1900.

Annie married a young man from Windsor, England, who had come to Richmond and worked on the grounds of the Van Lew home. They moved to Massachusetts, where he established a profitable wholesale produce business, and had eleven children, one of whom was the author's father-in-law.

Dorcas, Ben, Miss Lily, and Mr. Carmichael are products of the author's imagination, and have no history outside of this story, though a dressmaker was part of the route the messages traveled, and Annie did talk to a soldier hidden in the secret room.

Mary and Matt were real people, but what happened to them is not known to the author.

True to her promise, Annie never revealed the secret of the hidden room until years later, when she returned to Richmond after Auntie's death and again opened the door to the hiding place that had never been discovered by anyone else.

The beautiful home itself went out of the family after Auntie died, and was finally torn down in 1911, to be replaced by a brick elementary school which still stands on the site.

When Auntie died, the key to the code was found folded up tightly in the back of her watch. A copy of it is included here so that readers may have the fun of exchanging secret messages with their friends.

Elizabeth Van Lew's
Secret Code

6	R	N	B	H	T	X
3	V	1	U	8	4	W
1	E	M	3	J	5	G
5	L	A	9	0	I	D
2	K	7	2	Z	6	S
4	P	0	Y	C	F	Q
	1	3	6	2	5	4

The code is used by combining the number on the left of the row and the number on the bottom of the column in which the desired letter is. For example:

L=51; E=11; E=11; A=53; P=41; P=41; E=11; A=53; L=51; S=24. Broken up into groups of five numbers each, these letters would look like this: 51111

15341 41115 35124, and the translation would be LEE APPEALS. If there are not enough numbers to make a full group of five at the end, add as many zeros as necessary.